THE SHORT SELLER

Also by Elissa Brent Weissman

Nerd Camp

Standing for Socks

The Trouble with Mark Hopper

SHORT

Elissa Brent Weissman

Atheneum Books for Young Readers
NEW YORK LONDON TORONTO SYDNEY NEW DELHI

For Karina

A
atheneum

ATHENEUM BOOKS FOR YOUNG READERS $ An imprint of Simon & Schuster
Children's Publishing Division $ 1230 Avenue of the Americas, New York, New York
10020 $ This book is a work of fiction. Any references to historical events, real people, or
real places are used fictitiously. Other names, characters, places, and events are products
of the author's imagination, and any resemblance to actual events or places or persons,
living or dead, is entirely coincidental. $ Copyright © 2013 by Elissa Brent Weissman $
All rights reserved, including the right of reproduction in whole or in part in any form. $
ATHENEUM BOOKS FOR YOUNG READERS is a registered trademark of Simon & Schuster,
Inc. $ Atheneum logo is a trademark of Simon & Schuster, Inc. $ For information about
special discounts for bulk purchases, please contact Simon & Schuster Special Sales at
1-866-506-1949 or business@simonandschuster.com. $ The Simon & Schuster Speakers
Bureau can bring authors to your live event. For more information or to book an event,
contact the Simon & Schuster Speakers Bureau at 1-866-248-3049 or visit our website at
www.simonspeakers.com. $ The text for this book is set in Apollo MT. $ Manufactured
in the United States of America $ 0413 FFG $ First Edition $ 10 9 8 7 6 5 4 3 2 1 $
Weissman, Elissa Brent. $ The short seller / Elissa Brent Weissman. — 1st ed. $ p. cm. $
Summary: While seventh-grader Lindy Sachs is recovering from mononucleosis,
her father gives her access to his etrading account as a way to pass the time and she
discovers that she has a knack for buying and selling stocks. $ ISBN 978-1-4424-5255-8
(hardcover) $ ISBN 978-1-4424-5293-0 (eBook) $ [1. Stocks—Fiction. 2. Electronic
trading of securities—Fiction. 3. Best friends—Fiction. 4. Friendship—Fiction. 5.
Mononucleosis—Fiction.] I. Title. $ PZ7.W448182Sho 2013 $ [Fic]—dc23 $ 2012018632

PART ONE

Chapter 1
Sweet Spot

Lindy yawned and weighed the options on the table. She could start her homework, or she could start eating her plate of warm minicookies. Like there was even a choice. She stacked two of the cookies and bit into them together.

"Double-decker," Howe said. "You should eat one at a time so they last longer."

"Nah," said Lindy. She sucked a blob of melted chocolate off her finger. "That's no fun."

Howe slid into the booth opposite her and looked upside down at the books spread across the table. He barely even glanced at Lindy's plate of cookies, which didn't surprise Lindy but still amazed her. Somehow his dad being a baker had made Howe immune to the allure of sweets. Lindy thought if *her* dad worked at the Sweet Escape, she'd eat nothing but dessert.

"Are you ready for the math test on Friday?" Howe asked.

"Ugh, of course not." Lindy laid her head on her arm. "Steph's going to help me when she gets here. You should sit with us too. I can use all the help I can get."

Howe didn't try to hide his dislike for Steph. "I have to help my dad," he said, nodding toward the counter. "But if you have questions, you can call me later."

Lindy lifted her head, looked at her math book, and ate her third cookie. "Expect a call."

The door chimed as it opened, and Howe slid out of the booth, which meant it was Steph who'd entered. She was decked out in winter gear, including gloves, scarf, hat, and long, puffy coat. The hood of her coat was up too, creating a spaceman-effect with just her eyes and nose visible. Her family used to live in Arizona, where it was always warm, so they prepared for the New Jersey winter the way they would a trip to Antarctica. Lindy knew Steph didn't wear all the layers just for warmth, either. She had never owned a coat or any winter accessories before moving, so now, three years later, the novelty still hadn't worn off.

"Hey, Lindy!" Steph said as she began removing layers. "Hello, Howard."

"Hey," Howe said. He stuffed his hands into the sleeves

of his gray Windbreaker, his only jacket, no matter the weather. "I have to go help my dad. Later, Lind."

"Bye."

Steph slid into the booth, piled her clothes next to her, and shook out her long brown hair. "Why does he always leave when I arrive?"

"Maybe because you call him Howard. He hates that name."

Steph smiled. "That's why I call him it." She helped herself to one of Lindy's cookies. "I stopped next door and picked up the new *Teen Power*," she said. "It's got five pages of quizzes."

"Let me see," Lindy said. She and Steph were suckers for quizzes. They liked ones that promised to predict your future, but even better were ones that claimed to interpret the present. "'Are You Too Stressed?'" Lindy read. "If the answer is yes, do you think my mom will let me stop doing chores?"

"Probably not. Parents never appreciate the truth of magazine quiz results."

"'What's the Best Hat for Your Face's Shape?'"

"Ooh," said Steph. "What do they suggest for a heart-shaped face? That's what I have."

Lindy looked at her friend and realized that her face

was kind of shaped like a heart, with her center-parted hair forming the perfect bumps at the top.

"What shape is my face?" she asked Steph.

Steph didn't even need to consider. "Oval."

"And Howe's?" Lindy asked.

"Circle."

Lindy looked at him behind the counter and saw that Steph was right. His face was round, while her own was longer. Clearly, Steph had given this some thought before. "Impressive," she said. She went back to the magazine. "'Who's Your Celebrity Twin?' I hope those answers are better than 'What Is Your Spirit Animal?'"

"Shh!" Steph said, grabbing the magazine back from Lindy. "We promised to never speak of our spirit animals."

It was true; the results were too humiliating. Steph's was a sperm whale, which was embarrassing on multiple levels, and Lindy's was a bull, which Lindy thought was exactly that.

"Here we go," Steph said. "'Are You Really Best Friends?'"

"We know the answer to that," said Lindy. "How about 'Will You Be Able to Do a Triple Axel Next Week?'" she said. She and Steph were starting ice-skating lessons next week, and they'd taken to trying triple Axels in their living rooms, in the hallway at school, and even as they walked down the street.

"We know the answer to that!" Steph said. "We're going to be naturals."

"Okay, then," said Lindy. "Do they have 'Are You Going to Pass the Math Test on Friday?'" She frowned. "I think I know the answer to that, too."

Steph sighed and put the magazine away. "All right," she said. "Let's work on the homework."

But the minute Steph started talking through the first problem, Lindy began to lose focus. Something about numbers just made her zone out. She tried to concentrate, but she found herself wishing she could lie down right there in the booth and fall asleep.

"Hey."

Lindy blinked. Howe was standing at the side of the table, and he was holding a paper plate full of chocolate-chip cookies that were a deep brown.

"Do you want these?" he asked. "This whole tray got kind of burnt, and my dad was going to throw them away, but he said you could have them if you want."

"We don't need your cast-off cookies, Howard," said Steph.

"I wasn't offering you," Howe said. "I was offering Lindy."

Lindy looked at the cookies. "Thanks," she said, "but that's okay."

Steph smiled sweetly, but Howe just stared at Lindy. "Are you okay, Lind?"

"Yeah," she said, "I'm just really tired for some reason."

"Too tired for free cookies?" Howe said.

"No one wants your burnt cookies, Howard," said Steph.

Lindy rubbed her eyes. She wasn't in the mood to listen to them argue, and she certainly wasn't in the mood to focus on homework. "I think I'm going to go home. I'll call you guys later."

Steph pouted. "You're just going to leave me here?" she said.

"Leave you here, in the Sweet Escape, surrounded by deliciousness?" Lindy laughed as she filled her backpack. "I think you'll survive."

On her way out, she held the door open for Cassie, another girl from their class, and they smiled at each other.

"Hey, Cassie," Lindy heard Howe say. "Do you want these cookies? They're a little burnt, but you can have them for free."

"Serious?" said Cassie. "Awesome!"

Chapter 2

Down-and-Out

When Lindy tackled the math again after dinner, she was too tired to even be frustrated. She stared at the page until her eyes started to blur. Then she blinked, and the words and numbers came back into focus. But it didn't matter; they made as little sense in focus as they did blurry. She just wanted to go to sleep.

Her sister, Tracy, squeezed past on her way to get a Twizzler. "You're *still* working on that?" she asked.

Lindy lowered her head on to her paper. "I'm just no good at math." She lifted her head and slumped back into her chair, her forehead smudged with ink.

"You're not good at keeping pen off your head either," Tracy said. She rubbed Lindy's forehead with her hand as she passed again, and Lindy didn't even bother knocking it away.

"You're not bad at math," her mother said from the kitchen.

"I'm not *good* at it," Lindy said. "I wish everyone would stop telling me I am."

"They tell you because you are. You're even in the advanced class. Math just doesn't come quite as easily to you as everything else does, Melinda, so you have to try a little harder with it."

Lindy laid her cheek on her homework, not caring about adding more ink to her face. It was just taken for granted that she was good at math because she was good at all the other subjects. Last year when she did too poorly on the test to qualify for advanced math in seventh grade, her parents and teachers had decided that it must have been a fluke since her other scores were so high, and she was put into the advanced class, anyway. "It doesn't matter how hard I try," Lindy said to the crease of her book. "Math just doesn't make any sense to me." She rotated on to her chin and looked at her mother. "Can I go to bed? I'm really, really tired, and my throat kind of hurts."

"Maybe that's because you spent forty-five minutes on the phone with Steph, even after you hung out with her at the Sweet Escape," said Tracy.

"Whatever," Lindy murmured. "Like you *never* talk on the phone."

"Um, no, I don't," said Tracy. "Talking is so junior high. I text."

"Girls," said their mother.

Tracy shrugged, stuck her Twizzler between her teeth so she could use both thumbs to type on her cell phone, and walked down the hall to her room.

Mrs. Sachs wrinkled her forehead with a mixture of concern and suspicion. "You do look a little out of it. But it's only eight thirty," she said. "Keep at it for fifteen minutes. I bet you can knock out the whole page."

Only if I were good at math, Lindy thought. She sighed and reread the third problem.

Her dad came into the kitchen and searched the pantry. "I saw Tracy with a Twizzler," he said.

Tracy, whose bedroom door was mysteriously soundproof when she was being called for dinner or asked to help with chores, reacted immediately. "You can have *one*, Dad! I had to clean the bathroom *twice* to make Mom buy Twizzlers."

"A clean bathroom and Twizzlers in the house," he said with a wink at Lindy. "Win-win for us."

Lindy gave him a half smile and looked back at problem number three.

Mr. Sachs downed his Twizzler in two bites. Then he

picked up the phone, dialed a number, and shook his head. "Jim's not picking up his phone. I need to get the name of that stock I was telling you about"—he waited another few seconds before hanging up—"but he's not picking up."

"So? Talk to him tomorrow at work."

"That could be too late. The sooner we buy, the more money we'll make."

"So ask him first thing in the morning, and then buy it at work."

"I can't. The trading website is blocked at work, so I can't place the order until tomorrow night when I get home, and by then the stock market will be closed, and so we won't buy until Wednesday morning, and by then the price might have doubled."

Lindy looked up from her page of math problems. "What are you guys talking about?"

"Nothing," said her mother.

"Stock," said her father. "This guy at work was telling me about a company whose stock is really low but going up quickly. I wanted to buy some, but I don't remember the name, and he's not picking up his phone."

"What do you mean 'buy stock'?"

"Don't worry about it," said her mom. "Focus on your math."

"When you buy stock, you buy shares in a company," her dad explained. "They cost a certain price per share, and you can buy as many shares as you want. Then if the price of the stock goes up, you can sell your shares, and you make money."

"So the price changes?" Lindy asked.

"Right, it changes all the time. Jim told me shares of this particular company have a low price right now, so that's why I want to buy before it goes up."

Lindy wrinkled her ink-covered forehead. "Could the price go down?" she asked.

"It could," said her father. "There's always that risk when you buy stock."

Lindy thought. "So if it goes down, would you lose money?"

"If you sell it after it goes down, yes," he said. "Say you buy one share for five dollars, and then the price goes down to four dollars, and you sell your one share—"

"You'll lose a dollar," Lindy finished.

Lindy's mother patted her on the back. "And you said you're not good at math."

Lindy's shoulders sank. Why did she have to be reminded about math? "It's been fifteen minutes," she said. "I can't stay awake anymore. I'll finish this in homeroom tomorrow."

"Lindy . . ." But her mother sighed when she saw the dark half circles under Lindy's eyes. "All right, sweetie. Get a good night's sleep."

"Thank you." Pulling herself up from the table felt like pulling a towel out of a bucket of water. She leaned over to kiss her mother good night and almost lost her balance.

"Whoa, Lindy," her mom said. "You really don't feel well, do you? Let me feel your forehead."

"I'm fine," Lindy said, leaning away. "I just need to go to sleep." She said good night to her dad, who was trying unsuccessfully to reach Jim again, walked into her room, and fell onto her bed. *I should change into my pajamas,* she thought. But her next thought was that she had to remember to give a box of burnt cookies to her Hebrew school teacher or else her grandfather would fine her four dollars. The part of Lindy's brain that was still awake told her that she should at least get under the covers before she began to have weird dreams about burnt cookies and Hebrew school, but the other part said, *Who cares?*

And so her parents found her an hour later: lights on, jeans on, on top of the covers, fast asleep.

Chapter 3
Feeling Bearish

"Are you going to school?"

Lindy pulled her eyes open and lifted her head. She glanced at the clock. Seven o'clock. She looked in the doorway and saw Tracy fully dressed: coat, book bag, and everything. Then she looked at herself and realized she, too, was fully dressed, in her outfit from yesterday. "Oh man," she said.

"Is Lindy up?" Their mother pushed passed Tracy and sat down on the edge of the bed. "How are you feeling, honey?"

Lindy thought for a second. "Tired."

"Still?" said Tracy. "You just slept for, like, fifteen hours."

Their dad appeared in the doorway behind Tracy. "I guess neither of our daughters is good at math."

"Very funny, Dad."

"My throat still kind of hurts," said Lindy.

This time she couldn't get away from her mother feeling her forehead. "You do feel a little hot. Does anything else hurt? Your stomach? Do you feel achy? Is it the flu?"

"No, I think I'm okay." Lindy tried to swallow, but it felt like her throat was clogged. "Just my throat. And I'm still tired."

That was enough for her mother. "Go back to sleep," she said. "I'll call the school. And Dr. Gupta. I have an important meeting this morning, but I can come home around noon and take you then. I wonder if I can cancel that meeting. . . . Unless you can stay home, Gary?"

"I'm meeting with a client at ten," her dad said.

"I can stay home with her!" Tracy volunteered.

"Good try," said their mother, "but you'd better leave for school or you'll be late."

"I don't mind being late," said Tracy. "Anything to help my poor, sick baby sister."

"What a generous person you are," said her dad. "Totally selfless."

"I'm fine," said Lindy. "No one needs to stay home with me."

"You"—Mrs. Sachs pointed at Tracy—"get to school. You"—she rubbed Lindy's back—"put on some pajamas and go back to sleep. I'll come home as early as I can. Everyone"— she stood up—"out."

Today is backwards day, Lindy thought as she opened her pajama drawer and pulled out a pair of flannel pants and a T-shirt. *I put on my pajamas in the morning and go to sleep. Maybe tonight I'll eat breakfast and go to school.*

Just standing up made her feel a little bit better, but then she tried to swallow and her throat felt like mud.

Tracy tapped on her door and stuck her head in. "Are you sure you don't want to tell Mom you'd like someone to stay home with you? I have a French presentation third period that I am totally fine missing."

Lindy didn't blame her—she, too, dreaded speaking in front of class. It could be kind of fun to spend the day at home with Tracy. Since all of Tracy's friends would be at school and unable to talk or chat online, the two of them would have the whole day with just each other. They could watch game shows and eat Twizzlers. It'd be like when their bedrooms were being redone and the two of them had had to sleep in the basement on couch cushions. That had been like a month-long slumber party.

But that was four years ago, when Tracy was ten and Lindy was only eight. And today Lindy felt more like slumbering than partying. "I'm okay," she said. "I don't think Mom would let you, anyway."

"Yeah," said Tracy with a frown. She caught a glimpse

of herself in Lindy's mirror. "Shame to waste this good hair day too. Feel better." She gave her hair one last fluff before taking off.

Lindy had just finished changing when her mother appeared in her sister's place. She held the phone in her right hand and covered the mouthpiece with her left. "Dr. Gupta isn't in today. Do you want to see Dr. Favery?"

Lindy wrinkled her nose. Dr. Favery was probably twice as old as Dr. Gupta, called her "little missy," and smelled like creamed spinach.

Her mother wrinkled her nose in return. "I'm with you," she whispered. "I'll make the appointment for tomorrow?"

Lindy nodded and shrugged. Now that she'd been standing for a few minutes, she was ready to lie down again. She crawled back under the covers. But as quickly as her mother vacated her doorway, her father filled it. "Taking the day off?" he asked.

Lindy nodded. She thought about Steph, who once confessed to her that she'd faked being sick to make her parents pay more attention to her than her younger brothers. It *was* kind of nice having everyone checking in on her; if only she were feeling well enough to appreciate it.

"I know you're tired," her dad said. He closed the door behind him, sat down by Lindy on the bed, and rubbed his beard. Then he got a look like he was figuring something out. "I just had an idea," he said in a low voice with a glance at the door. "Since you're going to be home all day, could you do me a favor?"

Lindy raised her eyebrows. She didn't feel like doing much of anything, but the way her dad asked—like he'd suddenly remembered he was supposed to invite her to join a secret club—made her curious. "What is it?" she asked.

"Remember how we were talking about that stock last night?" he said. "If I call you from work and tell you the name of it, can you log in to the trading site for me and buy it?"

"Oh," said Lindy. "Okay."

"Okay!" said her dad. He stood up and clapped his hands. "Let me go get the laptop to show you how to do it." He left for only a few seconds, and when he came back the website was already up, and he had a piece of paper full of hand-written information. Lindy had a feeling he hadn't only just thought of this idea like he'd said.

"So this is the website," he said. "I'll leave it open here on the laptop, but just in case you navigate away or it times out, I wrote the URL down over here on this piece of paper."

Lindy nodded. She might have been bad at math, but she was good with computers. She rarely got to use her dad's laptop rather than the old desktop that was in the family room. Another perk of being sick, she realized, was that everyone brought everything to her. She thought about those kids at school who were always absent for one illness or another, and she wondered if they were really sick or just faking.

"Here's my log-in information: username and password. I know I don't have to tell you, Lind, but this is strictly confidential. More so than my other passwords."

"I know, Dad."

"Honest, Lindy. This is like a bank account. We have a lot of money in here. No one can know this password."

After receiving Lindy's assurance that she wouldn't do anything with the log-in information besides log in, he showed her how to buy stock. "You type the stock symbol in here. That's what I'll call and tell you. And then you put in the number of shares here. I'll tell you that, too. Then you press this order button, right here. Got it?"

"Got it."

"And then you log out like this."

"Got it," Lindy said with a yawn.

"Thanks, honey." Mr. Sachs kissed her forehead, tickling her with his beard. "I'll just put the laptop over here, right on your desk."

Lindy's mother returned carrying a shoe box filled with stuff: a heating pad, a sleeve of saltines, and a teacup with tea bag. "I brought this for you," she said. "We don't have one of those fancy breakfast-in-bed trays, so I just put it in this. And you'll have to go to the kitchen to make tea, since I didn't want to put boiling water in this shoe box."

Her dad got the portable phone and added it to the box. "Just in case," he said with a wink.

"Good thinking," said her mom. "We'll call you. And you call us if you start to feel worse. Do you have everything you need?"

Lindy thought, *What I really need is for you guys to leave so I can go to back to sleep.* But she said, "I think so. I'm really fine."

"And if she doesn't have something right here," her dad pointed out, "I think she knows where to find it. How long have you lived here, Miss Sachs? Ten years now?"

"Twelve," Lindy said with a small smile.

"Twelve?" her dad said with feigned shock. "We must be charging too little rent." He put his arm around his wife. "Let's let her sleep."

When her parents finally did leave, Lindy stretched out and sank into her mattress.

$ $ $

Lindy woke up a couple hours later when her dad called to give her the stock information. She climbed out of bed, pulled up the trading website like he'd shown her, and purchased three hundred and fifty shares of BIHR. The site was full of numbers and colored symbols, which made Lindy glad she didn't have to go to math class today. Maybe she'd be sick until Friday, and then she wouldn't have to take the test. She went to the bathroom, struggled through swallowing a couple saltines, and went back to sleep.

The next time she woke up, it was because her mother was stopping in during her lunch break to check on her. Lindy got out of bed and had a cup of tea while her mother ate lunch, then she lay on the couch and settled in to watch some TV after her mom went back to work. She managed to stay awake all through *Deal or No Deal*, *I Love Lucy*, and two episodes of *The Cosby Show*, but then she drifted off again. She slept soundly on the couch the entire afternoon until she heard the banging of pots that signaled dinner.

"She lives!" Tracy announced when Lindy entered the kitchen. "The curse has been lifted."

"It's five forty-five?" Lindy said.

"Yeah, and some people have had to do chores instead of sleeping," said Tracy. "What time have you been sleeping since?"

"I think *Ellen* was on."

Tracy, who had a working memory of the *TV Guide*, said, "Three? And Mom said you were sleeping all morning. What is going on?"

"I don't know," Lindy admitted. "And I'm still kind of tired. Like, I could go back to sleep right now."

"Maybe you're going into hibernation. You could be part bear." Tracy cocked her head. "You do kind of look like a bear."

"Stop it. I do not."

"It's not a bad thing. Bears can be cute. I mean, *you* don't look like one of the cute kinds, but they can be."

"Mom!" Lindy's voiced cracked on the *ah*, and she whimpered and rubbed her throat.

"Tracy!" their mother shouted from the laundry room. "Leave your sister alone. She's not feeling well."

"That means I'm allowed to bother you once you're better," Tracy said with a smirk.

Lindy stuck out her tongue. "I'll breathe on you," she threatened.

"And then I'll get to stay home and sleep and watch *Ellen* while *you* have to empty the dishwasher and be nice to me. . . ." Tracy opened her arms wide. "Breathe away."

The doorbell rang before either of them could do anything.

"Ask who it is before you open it!" yelled their mother.

Tracy rolled her eyes. "Yeah," she said to Lindy, "because a serial killer is really going to say 'It's a serial killer!' just because I asked."

Nonetheless, she said, "Who is it?" and a muffled voice called back through the door: "It's Steph!"

Tracy went back into the kitchen, and Lindy opened the door.

"Hey!" said Steph. "Where were you today?"

"Sick," said Lindy. "I slept pretty much all day."

"Lucky." Steph's shoulders sank inside her coat, but it hardly made a dent on her outerwear shell. "We're running late for piano, so my mom will start honking if I'm here more than five seconds, but I brought you your work." She handed her a stack of papers. "Well, I brought you math and English and social studies. Howard's bringing the rest."

Steph's mother tapped the horn twice, and Steph shook her head inside her hood. "Told you," she said. "Do you think you'll be in school tomorrow?"

"I don't know. I think I have a doctor's appointment in the morning."

"Well, call me later. I have to tell you what happened at lunch." She spread her hands, suggesting that what happened at lunch was *big*.

"Okay, but if I don't, it's because I'm asleep, and my throat really hurts."

Steph's mother leaned on the horn. "Bye," said Steph.

"Bye," said Lindy. "Have fun at piano."

Steph waved a mittened hand as she ran down the steps and into the car.

Lindy took her stack of work into her room and began sorting through it before dinner. A whole social studies chapter, an English practice essay, and four math dittos with problems she wasn't there to learn how to do. . . . Now she remembered the bad part about missing school. She wondered what had happened at lunch that Steph had to tell her. Howe probably wouldn't know. Without Lindy there, he wouldn't have sat at Steph's table. And even if he had, he probably wouldn't have realized anything was happening or that it was a big deal.

Lindy's eyelids became heavy, but she forced them open. "Come on," she said aloud. "You have to stay awake until tonight." She knew that if she had any chance of attaining that goal, she'd better stay away from the social studies chapter. Math would probably keep her awake with frustration, but she didn't need that right now. *English it is,* she thought.

She'd only written a quick outline of her essay when

she heard the garage door open. She knew her dad's arrival schedule down to the second. He'd pull in, close the garage door, come into the house, kiss her mom hello, wash his hands, change into sweatpants, knock on Tracy's door, and then knock on Lindy's. Depending on how talkative Tracy was feeling, Lindy had between seven and eight minutes until dinner—just enough time to write the introduction for the essay.

Lindy had only finished the first sentence when she heard her dad's signature knock on her door. She looked at the clock, hoping it hadn't somehow taken six minutes to write one sentence. But no, her dad had changed his routine. He knocked again. "Come in," she said.

"Hi, Lind," he said, pushing open the door and closing it halfway behind him. "How are you feeling?"

Lindy shrugged. "Eh. How was work?"

"Fine." Mr. Sachs tapped his fingers on Lindy's dresser and looked around the room. "Oh yeah!" he said as though remembering. "Did you manage to buy that stock this morning?"

Lindy nodded. "Yeah, I did it right when you called."

"Great! Why don't we see how it did today?"

"Okay. The laptop's right there on the floor."

Her dad turned it on and logged in to the trading site. He whistled while it loaded. Then he inhaled sharply and threw his hands in the air. "Yes!" he shouted. "It's up forty percent!"

Percentage was one of those things Lindy couldn't really grasp. "Up is good, right?" she said.

"Up is good, yes, and up forty percent is *great*. No, it's *spectacular*."

"But forty percent . . . ," Lindy said, unable to join in the excitement until she grasped the meaning of it. "Fifty percent is half, right? So forty percent doesn't seem that good."

Her dad moved the computer from his lap and stood up. "What's forty percent of a hundred?" he asked.

That seemed too easy, and Lindy hoped it wasn't a trick. She hesitated before saying, "Forty?"

"Right. Any percentage of a hundred is itself. Forty percent of a hundred is forty. Eleven percent of a hundred is eleven. Lindy percent of a hundred is Lindy."

Lindy rolled her eyes. "Dad."

"Okay. So let's say we bought one share for one hundred dollars. Now it's up forty percent, which is how many dollars?"

"Forty," Lindy repeated. "But forty is *less* than a hundred."

"But it's *up* forty percent. So we take that forty percent—forty dollars—and then *add* it to a hundred. Which makes . . ."

Lindy began to get it. "A hundred and forty dollars."

"Right! So it's like you bought a"—he looked around the room to pick an object—"backpack for one hundred dollars this morning. And then right now the price of that backpack is up to one hundred and forty dollars. You could sell the backpack right now and make forty bucks."

"And forty percent is pretty good for a stock to go up in one day?"

"Pretty good? It's downright spectacular. And we didn't just buy one share—or one backpack, say. We bought three hundred and fifty backpacks."

Lindy's eyes got large. "So we could sell all those backpacks and make forty bucks on *each* of them?"

"We could make forty *percent* on each of them, yep. It wouldn't be forty dollars on each because the shares weren't a hundred dollars to start. But we'll still make forty percent, and that's because you bought it at just the right time. If you waited until the afternoon to buy that hundred-dollar backpack, it might have cost, say, a hundred and twenty dollars, and then we would have made only twenty bucks."

"I get it!" Lindy said. "And if I wasn't home to buy it this morning, and you had to buy it right now, it would cost a hundred and forty bucks. So we got a good deal."

"We got a *great* deal, Lindy Hop." He pulled her head into his stomach and gave her a big kiss. "Thank you."

Tracy cleared her throat in the doorway. "I know you're having some sort of father-daughter moment," she said, "but it's been a lot more than eight minutes since the garage door opened, and you're not even in your sweatpants yet, Dad. When are we going to eat?"

Chapter 4

MONO

Despite her best intentions to finish the English essay, to call Steph, to take a long bath, and to stay awake, Lindy fell asleep shortly after dinner. She didn't wake up when Steph called the house, or when Howe rang the doorbell, or when her dad slipped into her room and put the homework Howe'd brought on her desk. And despite sleeping almost thirteen hours, she still had a hard time pulling herself out of bed when her mother woke her in the morning.

Dr. Gupta barely even had to examine her before announcing that Lindy most likely had mononucleosis.

"I was afraid it might be mono," said Mrs. Sachs.

"You were?" said Lindy. "Why were you afraid? What's mono?"

ELISSA BRENT WEISSMAN

"Mono," explained Dr. Gupta, "is a viral infection that gives you a sore throat and makes you very tired."

"That sounds like me," said Lindy. "Is it bad?"

"Not that bad," said the doctor, "but it takes a while to go away. You could be out of commission for a few weeks."

"Weeks?" said Lindy. "What about school? And I'm supposed to start ice-skating lessons on Monday."

"I can't imagine you'll feel up to ice-skating," Dr. Gupta said. "You'll probably feel too tired to go to school for a while, am I right?"

"You mean I'll feel *this* tired for weeks?"

Dr. Gupta nodded. "I'm going to have the nurse draw some blood so that we can make sure it's mono. We'll do a strep test, too. Sit tight until the results come in. Get plenty of rest—no need to worry that she's sleeping too much, Mom—and take some Tylenol if you're feeling achy. No sharing food or drinks, Lindy. Mono's very contagious, especially through saliva. I'll be in touch in a few days."

"Is there medication, then?" her mother asked.

Dr. Gupta shook her head. "If she's got strep, too, I can give her something for that. But mono's viral, so there's nothing you can do but wait it out."

Chapter 5
Realization

When Dr. Gupta called a couple days later to report that Lindy did, in fact, have mononucleosis and also strep throat, it came as no surprise. Lindy had been spending three-quarters of every day sleeping. Her parents would wake her in the morning before they left for work to say good-bye, and she'd stay up for a couple hours reading or watching TV. Then she'd go back to sleep until around dinnertime, when she'd take a bath, talk to Steph or Howe online, and try to do some of the mounds of schoolwork she was missing.

Without school or Hebrew school or being awake to watch prime-time TV, there was nothing separating the days, and the whole first week of being sick blended into a big, drowsy lump. But then, on Tuesday, exactly one week from the day Lindy first stayed home sick and purchased three hundred and fifty shares of BIHR for her dad, Lindy finally felt well enough to get out of bed and take her bath in the morning. That was when things started to change.

Rejuvenated from her early bath, Lindy didn't put her pajamas back on. Instead, she put on a pair of sweatpants and a hooded sweatshirt. It wasn't jeans, but it still made her feel more like a real person than she'd felt in a week.

Tired of tea but unable to swallow anything cold, she stuck a mug of water in the microwave and figured she'd drink it plain. She leaned against the counter and stared at the cup going around in the microwave. The steady motion and low hum began to hypnotize her. Her eyes were starting to close when the phone rang. She rubbed her face and got the cordless that was on the coffee table. "Hello?"

"Did I wake you?" asked her dad.

"No," Lindy said. "I'm actually feeling not as tired today."

"Oh good. You're on the road to recovery."

"I hope so. What's up, Dad?"

"I was wondering if you could do me a favor. You don't have to, but since you're up and you're at home. . . . Do you remember that stock site? Do you still have the log-in information?"

"Oh yeah," said Lindy, happy for something to do. "Let me go get the laptop."

"I got another good stock tip from Jim. I might want to buy some. Are you logged in yet?"

Settled on the couch with the computer in her lap and the mug on the coffee table, Lindy held the phone between her ear and shoulder and typed in the URL of the trading site. She entered the log-in information from her dad's instruction sheet and clicked enter. "It's loading. Hang on one second." Lindy put down the phone, pulled her hair into a ponytail, and picked the phone back up. "Okay."

"Okay. First I need you to look up a symbol to get a quote."

"What's a quote?"

"The stock quote. It tells you how much the stock costs right now. There should be someplace that says 'look up' or 'quote' or something like that."

Lindy sipped her hot water as she looked around the screen. In the upper right corner was a box that looked promising. "'Quick quote'?" she asked.

"Quick quote! Yes. Type in R-N-E-E."

Lindy typed it, and the quote showed up on the screen. "It says 'RNEE, twelve-point-three-two.' And then there's a little green triangle next to it."

"Twelve thirty-two," her dad said, but not to Lindy. "Is that about what you thought it'd be, Jim?"

"Do you want me to buy some?" Lindy asked. "Dad?" She

heard her dad and Jim talking, so she opened a new tab and logged into her e-mail account. A get-well e-card from her grandparents, a forwarded joke from Cassie, and an e-mail from Howe, sent just a few minutes ago.

LinD—

It's library day in science. We need to do Internet research for our project, so the librarian started by teaching us how to use a mouse. Are you really sick or did you just know this was coming?

Lindy laughed, which made her throat burn. Those library computer sessions were completely useless even for Lindy, and she wasn't nearly as big a genius with computers as Howe. She hit reply and typed quickly.

Howe—

I had to get sick at the worst time. . . . Now I'll never know how to use a mouse! You should do your research on why library teachers think kids don't know how to use computers!

"Lindy?" said her dad.

"I'm here." She clicked to switch back to the trading site.

"So RNEE's at twelve thirty. I'm going to have you buy some."

"Okay."

Another chat message popped up in the corner of the screen, this one from Steph. Lindy responded as quickly as she could.

AZgirlinNJ: LINDY!!!! i am in library DYING without u!!!!!

Lindyhop123: hi! yes! i am so over being sick

AZgirlinNJ: r u ready to ice skate? i am dreaming about triple sow cows (how do u spell that???)

Lindyhop123: no clue. hang on a sec, on phone with dad

"Do you remember how to buy?" Lindy's dad asked. "The instructions should be on that sheet I gave you."

"Yeah . . ." Lindy clicked to drag the chat box out of the way, but the computer was thinking, so she clicked again. The second she clicked, the computer came back into action, the chat was gone, and she'd accidentally hit the refresh button on the trading site. "Uh-oh," she said.

"What?" her dad asked.

"I reloaded it by accident, and something changed. I messed it up."

"What do you mean you 'messed it up'? What changed? Did you buy something?"

Lindy looked at the screen and started to breathe heavily. The symbol was the same, but the number was different. This was like in math class, when she zoned out for a second and looked back at the board to find the number in the problem was totally different. The quote had changed from 12.32 to 11.89, and Lindy had no idea how it happened. She hit the refresh button again and closed her eyes, hoping it would change back. But when she opened her eyes it was different again; this time 11.60.

"Lindy, what does it say?" her dad asked.

"It still says 'quick quote' and it still says 'RNEE.' But I hit the refresh button, and it changed from twelve thirty-two to eleven eighty-nine, and then I hit it again and it changed to eleven sixty."

"Oh. It went down to eleven sixty," her dad said as though reporting the weather.

"I'm really sorry, Dad. I swear I didn't do anything but refresh the page."

Her dad chuckled. "That's right," he said. "You refreshed the screen, and it's showing you the most up-to-date quote. The price changed, that's all. It went down from twelve thirty-two to eleven sixty."

Lindy still wasn't convinced that she hadn't done something wrong. She remembered her dad saying something about how the price of a backpack could go up a lot in one day, but she thought that meant in one day, not in one second. "It changes *that* quickly?"

"Yep. Hit it again. I bet it changed again."

Lindy moved the cursor over the refresh button and hesitated with her finger over the touchpad. She clicked. "Eleven seventy-five," she said.

"Okay, it's starting to go back up. That's good. We're going to buy some and hope it goes *way* up. And then we'll sell it and make lots of money. Okay?"

Lindy felt herself relax. "Okay." She followed the instructions on the sheet and purchased three hundred shares of RNEE at $11.90 per share, confirming each step with her dad before clicking to send it through.

Then, when she put the order through, the page refreshed and she saw that the price had already gone up to $12.10. "Dad," she said, "it's at twelve ten. So if we sell those shares we just bought right now, we'll make money, right?"

"We will, but not that much money. We bought it at eleven ninety, and now it's at twelve ten. So we'll only make twenty cents per share."

"But we bought three hundred shares." She tried to do some math in her head, then pulled up the computer's calculator and did the multiplication on there. "So we'd make six thousand cents . . . which is . . . sixty dollars." Her eyes widened. It would take her three whole afternoons of babysitting to make sixty dollars, and here she made it in ten seconds, just by clicking a few buttons.

"We would make sixty bucks," her dad said. "But we're holding out for more—we're in this for the long-term. In a few months, or a year or two, it could double; triple, even. And in ten years, it could be selling for a hundred dollars a share—who knows."

"We're going to hold on to it *that* long?" Lindy asked.

"Maybe not that long. If it goes up a lot this week, maybe we'll sell some and make a quick buck. We'll see. But the safest thing to do is hold on to stocks for a while, because they go up and down quickly in the short-term—like you saw—but in the long-term, they tend to go up."

Lindy was only half listening to what her dad was saying. She hit refresh and saw that RNEE had gone up to 12.20. Then she hit it again, and it went down to 12.17. "But you *could* buy stock and then sell it really quickly and make money, right, Dad?"

"It's possible," her dad said. "But it's— Hi, Susan. What do you need?"

Lindy's fingers began tingling, and she felt energized from the neck up, like her brain was coming to life.

"I've got to get back to work, Lind," her dad said. "See you later."

"Bye," said Lindy. Her dad hung up, but she sat staring at the computer in a halfway state between waking and sleep. She hit refresh once more, and the price of RNEE was up to 12.31. She didn't notice when the phone started beeping or when Howe's and Steph's chat messages started flashing. She just sat looking at the trading screen, her mind working and the cursor stationed over the reload button.

Chapter 6

Initial Public Offering

The next night was supposed to be Lindy's first ice-skating lesson, and she held out a small hope that she'd be able to go, even though her parents didn't say a word about it during dinner. When she finished eating, she changed into the ice-skating outfit she'd spent a good portion of the afternoon selecting, and she walked back into the kitchen carrying the box with her new, white ice skates, the leather still stiff and smooth.

Her mom saw her and frowned. "You're not well, Lindy," she said. "There's no way I'm letting you go ice-skate."

"But I feel fine," Lindy lied. "I did homework for two hours. And it's not like I'm going to go to sleep before eight, anyway. I might as well be ice-skating instead of sitting here."

"You've got mono, Lind," said her dad.

"And strep throat," her mother reminded her. "That's not fully out of your system yet."

"But the strep medication made it so I'm not contagious anymore. Dr. Gupta said."

"Dr. Gupta also said you're not allowed to ice-skate."

"No," Lindy said quickly. "Dr. Gupta said I probably wouldn't be feeling well enough to ice-skate. She didn't say I wasn't *allowed* to ice-skate. That's not the same."

"She's right," said Tracy, who was passing through the kitchen. Her mother gave her a warning look, and Tracy raised her arms in surrender as she settled into a chair to follow the argument.

"Come on, Mom, please?" said Lindy. "How about I go, and if I'm feeling tired, I'll stop. You can stay the whole time, and I promise I'll leave if I don't feel well."

Her parents looked at each other, and Lindy thought that she might be gaining ground. "I've been looking forward to this for months," she said. "Steph's going. And you already bought the ice skates. Please?"

Her dad sighed and nodded at her mother.

Lindy inhaled and crossed her fingers.

But her mother leaned against the countertop. "I'm sorry, honey, but you can't go. We canceled your registration for the class."

Tracy let out a quiet gasp. Then she got up and walked quickly to her room.

"What?" said Lindy. "When? Why?"

"On Saturday," her mom said. "If you don't cancel forty-eight hours before the first class, you have to pay for the entire session. You couldn't have gone tonight no matter what, honey. You're still very contagious. But we'll register you for the next session that starts in March."

Lindy started to cry, and her throat felt even muddier than it had all week.

"The next winter Olympics isn't for four years, so two months won't affect your chances," her dad said.

Letting the tears drip down her face and on to her shirt, Lindy realized that she didn't feel well enough to go to ice-skating, anyway. She was mad, but not really at her parents for canceling the whole session—she knew the lessons were very expensive; that's why it had taken so much work to get them in the first place. To get down to it, she was mad at her body for making her too tired to do *anything*. "I haven't been out of this house in a whole week," she said, the words breaking on her sobs. "I don't feel well, and I'm *bored*. Tracy goes to school and to Hebrew High and volleyball and to friends' houses and the mall." She breathed in a shaky breath. "And I'm stuck doing *nothing*. It's not fair."

By now she was sobbing and blubbering and soaking wet, and—she could almost laugh—exhausted. Her dad handed her a dish towel, and she wiped her face with it.

Her mother rubbed her back and said, "You'll feel better soon. You're better today than you were a week ago. You just need to make the most of your time at home." She snapped her fingers. "Tracy said her friend had mono and she took up knitting."

Even through her tears, Lindy's look made it clear that she was not about to take up knitting.

"Well, we'll keep thinking," her mom said.

Lindy sniffed and swallowed. "I'm going to bed."

Back in her pajamas and under the covers, Lindy got online and told Steph that she'd be going ice-skating alone.

AZgirlinNJ: noooooo u have to come!!!!

Lindyhop123: i wish i could. but i'm still sick. : (

AZgirlinNJ: can't u just go anyway? uv been sick forever and it's getting old

Lindyhop123: tell me about it. i can't wait to be better

AZgirlinNJ: will you b there next week?

Lindyhop123: no. my parents canceled the whole session

AZgirlinNJ: what??? that is so lame

Lindy realized that talking to Steph wasn't going to make her feel better right now. She told her to have fun at the lesson and closed the computer. Too angry to sleep and too tired to read, she sat in bed and stared at the stripes on her comforter, making her eyes blur the colors and separate them again.

Tracy knocked on her door and entered hesitantly. "Sucks about ice-skating," she said.

Lindy sniffed and nodded.

"Don't start knitting," said Tracy. "You're sick, not sixty."

Lindy giggled. "Did your friend really do it?"

"Jackie, yeah! She still does. She makes scarves and things. They're actually kind of nice."

The two girls looked at each other in silence for a few seconds.

"Anyway, I'm done with this." Tracy held out a copy of *Seventeen* magazine. "Do you want it?"

Stuck in the house, Lindy had no use for the "cute winter layers" and even less interest in figuring out the perfect shade of eye shadow for her sick, pasty skin tone, but she recognized a sisterly gesture when she saw one. "Really?"

"Yeah, take it. I've got more old ones in my room, too, when you're done. Just let me know if you want them." Tracy raised a finger. "*Ask me.* Don't you dare go in there."

Lindy smiled. "Thanks."

Tracy smiled back and shrugged. "Good night."

"Night."

Lindy tried to swallow and winced in pain. Crying was definitely no good for her throat. She flipped past the ads in *Seventeen* and found a quiz: "Discover Your Perfect Career!"

> *What would be your ideal way to spend a Saturday*
>   *afternoon?*
> *a. Curled up with a book.*
> *b. Hiking through the woods.*
> *c. Proving the Pythagorean theorem.*
> *d. Getting a beauty-counter makeover.*
> *e. Serving food at a homeless shelter.*

That one normally would have been a quick and easy *a*, but now that she was going to be curled up with books and mono for the foreseeable future, hiking through the woods sounded incredibly appealing. Still, you had to be completely honest with yourself in these quizzes—something it didn't seem Tracy was by the fact that there was a penciled circle around *e*. Lindy circled *a*.

A knock on her door drew her away from the quiz. This time it was her dad. "Sorry about the ice-skating, Lind. But since you're home for the evening and not knitting, do you want to check how the stock we bought is doing?"

She closed the magazine and tried to swallow again—it was a little easier this time. "Sure."

Her dad kissed her forehead and went to get the laptop. When he came back, he was already logged in to the site, but he hadn't clicked to display their positions yet. The cursor was over the positions button, and his finger was over the touchpad. "Are you ready?"

Lindy giggled. It was kind of suspenseful. "Not yet," she said. She made a show of taking a big breath, rubbing her eyes, and cracking her knuckles. "Okay."

Her dad cleared his throat, scratched his head, and tugged on his right ear.

"Okay, Dad. Are you ready now?"

"Hang on." Mr. Sachs tapped his stomach, pulled his beard, and did a vocal scale: "Me-me-me-me-ME-me-me-meeeeee."

Lindy laughed. "Come on, Dad! Click it."

"Just one more thing. I almost forgot about this one, but you have to do it before you check your positions." He put his hands beside his mouth and called so loudly that the glass of water on the nightstand quivered: "Ca-caw! Ca-caw!"

Lindy broke down in hysterics. "Dad!"

"Okay," he said calmly. "Let's check it."

The positions page was full of symbols and numbers, but Lindy only cared about the two lines with the stocks she had purchased. RNEE was at 15.20—up 27.7 percent—and BIHR was down a little from when she'd last checked, but still up 28 percent overall.

"Stupendous," her dad said quietly. "Absolutely stupendous."

"We're up *huge*, right, Dad?"

Mr. Sachs nodded. "We're up huge, all right. This column here shows the percentage that we're up. And then this column shows how much we're up or down in dollars."

Lindy looked closer. She'd been focusing on the two things she and her dad had talked about: the cost of one share, and the percentage change. She hadn't even noticed the other columns, the ones that had dollar amounts, even though they had dollar signs and everything. *Figures,* she thought. *I'm so dense at math, I always manage to miss half of the important information.* But with math problems she didn't really get why she had to use the numbers she did or even what she was missing when she missed big chunks of information. With stocks it was obvious; it was easier. Rather than thinking about how her three hundred shares of RNEE were now at 15.20 and had changed 27.7 percent, she could see it in real dollars.

"We spent three *thousand* five *hundred* dollars on RNEE?" she asked, pointing to the column that said, "cost."

"Yes, and now it's worth more than four thousand five hundred. See?"

Lindy followed the row to the next column, the one that made math much more convenient than it was in school. "So we're up nine hundred and ninety dollars." Just saying it—just forming the words and hearing them come out of her mouth—made her realize exactly how much money that was. *We made almost a* thousand *dollars,* she thought. If she made twenty bucks babysitting in one night, and she babysat four nights a month, and she got a cookie instead of a cupcake after school to save fifty cents, and she helped her neighbor rake leaves . . . All of that meant she could make about a hundred dollars in a month. If she did all of that for *ten* months, and she didn't spend a single penny of it, only then would she have saved a thousand dollars. That was nearly impossible. And here she was, making almost a thousand dollars in a couple of days. Her brain felt like it was fizzing.

"We made nine hundred and ninety dollars," she repeated.

"Not exactly," her dad said. "We're *up* that amount, yes.

But we won't actually make any money until we sell the stock. Then we'll make however much we sell it for. Get it?"

"Yeah. Let's sell it right now."

Her dad laughed. "We're in this for the long-term, Lind, remember? We're going to let it grow."

Why would you let it grow when you could sell it right now and make almost a thousand dollars? Lindy thought. That was like Howe, who sometimes brought one of his dad's delicious cupcakes with lunch. Lindy would keep looking at it as it sat on his tray for the entire period. Howe would eat his sandwich and yogurt and drink his milk without even glancing at the cupcake until he'd finished every crumb of everything else. Then, with only two minutes before the bell, he'd lick off the icing. And with only one minute to go, he'd take small, restrained bites, chewing each fully before taking another. Lindy did not get how he could be so patient. She always ate her dessert first, and in one or two big gobbles. It took all her willpower not to grab and devour Howe's cupcake too.

"Look at this stock here." Mr. Sachs pointed to a line of the chart that Lindy hadn't paid attention to before. "I bought this a month ago, see? And it's gone down two percent. It goes up and down, but in the long run it should go up slow and steady. Maybe I'll sell it in six years to help pay your college tuition."

Lindy's eyelids and mouth dropped down. "Six *years*?" In six years she'd be eighteen. Who knew *what* the world would be like then? She could be driving a flying car and telepathically telling her pet robot she'd like macaroni and cheese for dinner. Who knew if she could sell stock in six years? "We shouldn't wait six years to sell the ones I bought," she said. "We should sell them now and make nine hundred and ninety dollars."

"That's my Lindy Hop," her dad said with a smile. "Patient as always."

"I'm serious, Dad. That's easy money."

Her dad scratched his chin through his beard. "I'll tell you what," he said. "How about this: I'll give you one hundred dollars to buy and sell stock. You can buy whatever you'd like, and you can sell it whenever you'd like." ·

"Really?" said Lindy. "A *hundred* bucks?" That was probably the biggest allowance any kid would ever receive. Even Steph had less than that saved up, and her family was loaded.

"A hundred bucks. You'll have to think about what you want to buy and how much of it. You should probably do some research to see what's a good bet."

"So I could buy one hundred dollars of RNEE tomorrow morning and then sell it tomorrow afternoon and be rich?"

Her dad shrugged. "If it worked out that way. Or you

could spread it around to different stocks—diversify your portfolio to protect yourself from too much risk."

Lindy ignored that last part since she didn't know what it meant, but she knew her dad was saying she could spend it all on one stock or spend a little bit on lots of different stocks. "If I make money, can I buy stock with that money too?"

"You can, or you can keep it. Or you can let it grow until you can pay your own college tuition. But one hundred is all you get. Once you lose it, you need to start knitting."

Lindy looked at him sideways. "You're kidding, right?"

"About knitting, yes. Not about the money. I'll have to ask Mom, but I'm sure she'll agree." He was talking quickly now, becoming more animated, and Lindy could tell that he was really getting into his idea. "I'll set aside a hundred dollars for you in a special fund on the trading site. What do you think? Want to start investing?"

It wasn't ice-skating, but it was definitely more interesting than reading about winter accessories in Tracy's *Seventeen*. And it meant making money, which she wouldn't be able to do by babysitting or raking leaves while she was sick. And how often was it that a parent just offered a kid a hundred dollars and looked like he'd beg for her to take it? "I can buy and sell whenever I want?" she asked.

"Whenever you want."

ELISSA BRENT WEISSMAN

Lindy smiled. "Cool."

Her dad stood up and closed the laptop. "Cool indeed! Stupendous, actually. This hobby is going to be the envy of all your friends! I suggest you start researching."

Lindy let out a big, stretchy yawn.

"But first," her dad said, "I suggest you get some sleep." He patted her hand. "I'll talk to Mom and give you the signal when we're ready."

"What's the signal?" Lindy asked.

"The stock-checking signal. You know it." Her dad pushed out his chest and put his hands by his mouth. Then he shrieked with all his might: "Ca-caw!"

After he left and Lindy stopped laughing, she completed her quiz. She tallied up her answers and turned to page seventy-five to find out her dream career. "Business tycoon," it read. "You've got the drive and savvy to conquer the corporate world—and become filthy rich!"

Filthy rich business tycoon, Lindy thought before falling asleep. *Maybe.*

Chapter 7
Opening Call

Tracy sat on Lindy's bed when she got home from volleyball the next afternooon. "What's this I hear about you getting a hundred bucks?"

Lindy opened her eyes groggily. "Mmm?"

"I heard Mom telling Dad he could give you a hundred bucks."

Lindy edged out from under the covers. "Yeah, to buy stock."

"To buy *socks*?" said Tracy. "Who needs that many socks?"

"Stock," Lindy said, rolling her eyes and becoming more awake. "Like in the stock market. Online."

Tracy cocked her head. "Oh."

"Why? Did you hear that I'm definitely getting it?"

"Yeah, Mom said okay. Oh, and Dad left this weird

message on your door. I think he's losing it." She went to the door and brought Lindy a Post-it that said, "CA-CAW! CA-CAW!"

Lindy laughed and shook her head. It was the signal, all right.

"You know what that means?"

"It means I'm getting the money."

"I should get a hundred bucks too," said Tracy.

"What for? I need a hobby I can do from bed."

"And I need this new blow-dryer that has special ions to straighten your hair without frizz."

"You need a hundred-dollar blow-dryer?" Lindy asked.

"It's seventy-five, and yes. Leigh Anne tried it, and it really works. Her mom got it as a sample at her salon. It's not even in regular stores yet, but it's going to be really soon, and then it'll probably sell out right away."

"Why don't you just buy it yourself? You've got tons of money."

It was true. Tracy had been saving since second grade. Despite the number of sweaters in her closet, she was actually very careful about her spending.

"Yeah, I don't really want to spend seventy-five bucks on a blow-dryer. But if Mom and Dad are just giving out money, that's another story." She sighed. "Well, I'm out. Some of us have to do homework and go to Hebrew High, not just sit around and think about ways to spend a hundred bucks."

"I have to do homework," Lindy said, pointing to the pile of work on her desk. "Even though I'm too tired to get out of bed, and I feel like my throat is going to close up—"

"Yeah, yeah. Sick, mono, dying, I know." Tracy saluted. "Later, sis."

Lindy yawned again and leaned back into her pillow. But she wasn't going to go back to sleep today—she was allowed to buy stock! She could buy whatever she wanted and see what happened with it. She could hit the refresh button every three seconds, if it meant selling at the right time.

But first she had to figure out what stock to buy. *Something good,* Lindy thought. *Something that is going to go up quickly.* A good time to invest in a company, her dad had said, is when it's just getting starting and it's going to be big, or when it's going to introduce a new product or service that's going to be big. The key was to get in *before* everybody started buying something.

Lindy sat up with a jolt. "Trace!" she called.

Tracy appeared in her doorway a few seconds later. "Yeah?"

"That blow-dryer. You said it's not out yet, but once it is, you think everyone is going to want one for real?"

"Definitely," Tracy said. "Leigh Anne's mom is going to buy one for every person in her salon. It's supposed to be amazing for your hair."

"Who makes it?" Lindy asked. "What company?"

"Dream Dry," Tracy said as though she were really dreaming. "The Dream Dry 130-Z." She looked at her sister. "I've got to get one."

Lindy rubbed her hands together and asked Tracy to bring her the laptop. She had just found her first stock.

Chapter 8
Pairs Trading

Finding out the stock symbol for Dream Dry was simple. First she googled "find a stock symbol" and found a website that would give her the symbol for any company. So she typed in Dream Dry, and there it was: DDRY. As her dad would say, this was all going along stupendously!

Now she pulled up the stock trading website and logged in. She did a quote lookup for DDRY. The computer was being slow, so Lindy messaged Howe.

Lindyhop123: What would you do with thousands of $?

Whowhatwhenwherewhy: sea monkeys

Lindyhop123: lol!! what?

Whowhatwhenwherewhy: whoops sorry wrong message

Whowhatwhenwherewhy: hi lindy

ELISSA BRENT WEISSMAN

Whowhatwhenwherewhy: thousands of $ . . . hmm . . .

Lindyhop123: who are you talking to about sea monkeys?

Whowhatwhenwherewhy: steph

Lindy stared at the screen. Steph? Maybe, *maybe* Steph and Howe would be talking online, but it'd have to be quick and short, like "What's the science chapter for tonight?" or "Do you know how Lindy's doing?" But sea monkeys? That sounded like a real conversation, one between friends. You don't just start with sea monkeys; you have to be talking a little while for the conversation to go that way. Were Steph and Howe talking for a little while? To each other?

Lindyhop123: ur talking to steph?

Whowhatwhenwherewhy: yeah she's actually kind of cool

Lindyhop123: i know. i've been trying to tell you that forever. what made you realize?

Whowhatwhenwherewhy: don't know. without you around i have to talk to new people.

So now Steph and Howe were friends. That should be good. But it didn't feel like it. If they were going to talk, Lindy wanted it to be because the three of them were talking, not because she was replaced.

She shook her head quickly and regrouped. Now wasn't the time to think about it. Now was the time to become a millionaire by investing in Dream Dry.

She clicked back to the stock page, her mind flashing with images of what she'd buy with her earnings: her own ice-skating rink and personal coach; an inground swimming pool with a waterslide; a lifetime all-you-can-eat membership to the Sweet Escape. More stock, of course. And a Dream Dry 130-Z for Tracy to thank her for giving her the initial tip.

But those dreams evaporated when Lindy looked at the loaded page. One share of DDRY was $42.30. This was like a word problem from math class. It was like she wanted to buy cupcakes, and they cost $42.30 each. How many could she buy with one hundred dollars? She pulled up the computer calculator and did the division. When the answer popped up, it felt like her plans were sunk.

If she spent her whole hundred dollars, she could only buy two shares. Two. That wasn't very many.

Well, she reasoned, *if the price of the stock goes up to fifty dollars in an hour, and I have two shares, I'll make*—she went back to the calculator—*$7.70 per share, so $15.40 total.* That wasn't great, but it was something.

Ignoring the flashing chat from Howe and a new one

from Steph, she pressed the refresh button. DDRY changed from 42.30 to 42.34. She waited ten seconds and pressed it again. It changed to 42.29. "I don't think this is going to go up to fifty in an hour," she said aloud.

She opened Steph's chat, and without even reading the message, Lindy typed:

Lindyhop123: i need to buy a stock that's really cheap

AZgirlinNJ: what?

Lindyhop123: stock i'm buying stock, but i need a cheap one. any ideas?

AZgirlinNJ: no clue but listen to this

AZgirlinNJ: today in band cassie sat in the first seat b/c she forgot her glasses and needed to see mr. gilley

AZgirlinNJ: and tamara FREAKED OUT and started going off on how she is first clarinet and cassie has no right to sit there

AZgirlinNJ: so mr. gilley didn't know what 2 do and told cass 2 move even tho he knew she wouldn't be able 2 see

Lindyhop123: geez. that's so tamara. it's not like it was a concert or something. it was just class

AZgirlinNJ: i know!!! but there's more!!

Lindyhop123: wait. since when does cassie wear glasses?

AZgirlinNJ: oh yeah! i 4got u weren't there last week. she just

got them and dave made fun of her for it and he got sent
down 2 principal

Lindy yawned. She read through Steph's messages about how Amy, who was supposed to be Cassie's best friend, sat with Tamara at lunch, but it was hard to focus. Just last week she would have been all over this band gossip, but now that she was stuck at home, it was hard to see the point. By the time she got back to school, all this drama would be long forgotten, replaced by fresher, juicier news involving different people. And no matter how diligently she tried to keep up, she'd still be hopelessly behind, like she was with Cassie's glasses.

She went back to her Internet browser and searched for "cheap stocks" and got eleven million results. She searched for "how to pick stocks" and got fourteen million results.

AZgirlinNJ: so then renee was like "ok but i'm still trading lockers"
AZgirlinNJ: can u believe that??? she's crazy!!!

Trading lockers couldn't make you any money right from your own bed. Trading stocks could.

Lindyhop123: no way. she is. ok, gotta go

Lindyhop123: bye

She exited the chat program and maximized the browser page. Then she started to read.

Chapter 9
Day-Trading

Lindy spent the next morning in a blur of stock trades. She found a stock that cost only $1.16 per share, and she bought ten shares. She sold them thirty minutes later, when it was up to $1.25 share. It wasn't a big profit, but it felt good. Her confidence growing, she bought twenty-five shares of a stock that cost $2.03 a share, but it went down every time she hit refresh for twenty minutes, so when it went up, briefly, from $1.85 to $1.89 she sold it all, even though she took a loss.

After lunch and a half hour of English homework, she found a stock called FGY that had been steadily rising all morning and was now at $3.15 per share. After five minutes of talking herself into it, she took a deep breath, crossed her fingers on the touchpad, and put through an order for nineteen shares—almost sixty dollars' worth. She tried to stay awake to watch it, but her illness was putting up a strong fight, weighing down her eyelids and increasing the gravitational pull of her bed.

She awoke with a jolt when she heard the garage door open. *FGY!* she thought.

She reached for the laptop, but it wasn't on her nightstand. *FGY!* she thought again.

"Tracy!" she yelled. She could hear her talking on the phone through the wall.

"We should probably work on it at your house," Tracy said. "My sister has mono."

"Tracy!" Lindy said again.

"Yeah, right. She's only twelve," Tracy said into the phone. "I know it's called that, but that's because it's passed through saliva. You can get it from sharing a drink or something."

Lindy listened and looked for something to throw at the wall to get her sister's attention.

"Don't even say that," Tracy said. "If she kissed someone before me, I'll die."

Lindy stopped to register that statement. She smiled. Then she chucked her pillow toward the wall.

Her dad opened her bedroom door in time to see the pillow crash against the wall and land in a pile of dirty clothes. He raised his eyebrows.

"Sorry," Lindy said. "But Tracy took the laptop. Can you get it for me?"

Mr. Sachs kept his eyebrows raised. "Doesn't Tracy have her own laptop?"

"Yeah, but it's not here. Tracy's always taking things."

"Hold on a minute," Tracy said into the phone. She dropped it on her bed and walked to Lindy's doorway. "First of all, I can hear you, you know. Number two, you've got mono, not two broken legs. You can get out of bed and get things for yourself. And three, yes, I have my own laptop, so stop accusing me."

"Then who took it?" Lindy asked as her father backed away.

"I did," her mother replied, appearing in the doorway with the laptop in her hands. "It *is* technically mine."

"Well," said Mr. Sachs, "it's technically both of ours."

Lindy felt her face turning red. "Sorry, Mom. But do you think I can use it? I want to check something."

Mrs. Sachs handed Lindy the computer with a cautious nod. "I'm going to put in a frozen pizza. Dinner in fifteen minutes."

Tracy cleared her throat.

Lindy sighed. "Sorry for accusing you, Tracy."

"Not forgiven." Tracy started heading back to her room.

"Oh, Trace?" Lindy said innocently. "You know how you can hear me in your room? I can hear you, too. You know, talking about my mono and what causes it and everything." Trying not to smile, she opened the laptop and pulled up the browser.

Tracy took a moment to register the comment, then turned red herself and disappeared into her bedroom.

Mr. Sachs eased himself into Lindy's room and sat at the edge of her bed. "What'd you need to check, Lind? We're past the closing bell."

"What does that mean?"

"It means there's no more buying or selling for today. Market's closed."

Lindy opened her eyes wide. "It closes? What time does it close?" What if FGY was way up—or way down? She couldn't do anything about it because the market was *closed*?

"Four o'clock."

"Four o'clock!" said Lindy. "The mall is open till ten, but the stock market closes at four o'clock?"

Mr. Sachs laughed. "It's closed weekends, too. But it'll open tomorrow at nine thirty."

"Will the price of things be the same as when they closed?"

"For the most part. Sometimes stocks jump up or go down first thing in the morning, but they usually stabilize within an hour or so. And there's after-hours trading, but that shouldn't affect things too much."

"After-hours trading?" Lindy asked. "How do I that?"

Mr. Sachs laughed again. "You don't. What'd you buy?"

Lindy was silent while she logged into the site and waited for her positions to come up. She prayed that she didn't lose her sixty dollars while she'd been asleep. *I don't need to make a lot of money,* she thought, *but please, please, please don't be way down.*

The screen loaded. Lindy looked. There was FGY, and it had a little green triangle next to it. Relief flowed through her, pumping from her heart to her fingertips. Her eyes followed the line across to see just how much it had gone up. It was at $4.09. It had gone up ninety-four cents! Almost a whole dollar! Thirty percent! Her $59.85 had turned into $77.71!

"Hey," said her dad, peering over her shoulder. "You made seventeen bucks on FGY!"

Lindy grinned. "I did."

Her dad patted her on the back and left to complete his pre-dinner routine. Lindy sat smiling at her portfolio. *Good thing I was asleep,* she thought, *or else I might have sold it when it was only up fifty cents, or ten cents!* If only she'd spent her whole hundred dollars instead of just sixty dollars.

Then she'd have made thirty dollars instead of seventeen. And if she'd spent three thousand—what her dad had spent on that first stock she bought for him—she'd have made nine hundred dollars! *But I don't have three thousand dollars,* she reminded herself. *I have a hundred.* Then she looked at her day's transactions and smiled. *$115.26 now.*

Chapter 10
Uptick, Downtick

In three days, Lindy turned her $115 into $144. She also got three books in the mail from her grandma: *Investing for Teens*; *The Stock Market: An Introduction*; and *Buying Stock for Dummies*. The package included a note that said she found that last book to be the most useful one in the store; it wasn't meant to be an insult. A quick flip through proved that she was right, *Buying Stock for Dummies* was the best one. She spent all of Tuesday afternoon reading it, only falling asleep once, and only for two hours. Tracy saw her reading it and said, "I guess we know what Grandma thinks of you," but Lindy ignored her and kept reading about diversification.

The next morning looked grim for a while; her portfolio was down twelve percent at eleven o'clock. But then she put a stop-loss on TTKP and bought some extra FGY, and she was back ahead by the time she woke up for lunch at twelve thirty.

By the end of the week, she was feeling much less tired, and she only needed one short nap a day. She was going to go to the doctor on Tuesday to see if she was clear to start school again.

The news made her equally happy and nervous. She was excited to get back to her old life and her friends, especially now that Steph and Howe were getting along. But being in school would leave her very little time to make trades, and she was on a roll. When her dad got home from work, she mentioned that if she had a smartphone, she could keep up her hobby during the day. It seemed like he might actually consider it until her mom stepped in.

"Let me get this straight," her mom said. "Even though we've told you repeatedly that you can't have a cell phone until you're thirteen, you want us to get you a smartphone so you can make stock trades at school instead of paying attention in class."

Lindy's shoulders slumped. "Come on," she said. "I won't do it *during* class."

Tracy came out of her room. "What won't she do during class?"

"Use a smartphone to make stock trades," their dad said.

Tracy's mouth flew open. "No fair! I didn't even get my lousy regular cell phone until I was thirteen. If Lindy gets a smartphone, then I get a smartphone."

"No one's getting a smartphone," their father said with finality. "*I* don't even have a smartphone."

"And, Tracy," their mother added, "if you think your regular phone is so lousy, I'll be happy to take it away. No one says you have to have one at all."

"Never mind," Tracy grumbled.

At dinner, Lindy's parents had more bad news for her.

"I called the school today, and your math teacher thinks you're going to have a hard time catching up when you get back," her mom said.

Duh, Lindy thought. Between trading and reading about trading, she'd barely been keeping up with her English homework, let alone math. It seemed like she'd missed so much in math that she'd have to repeat the year. She imagined starting high school but having to take a bus over to the junior high for math class. The thought of it made her shiver. "That's because the math we do at school doesn't make any sense," she said, cutting into her chicken breast. "But I'm reading those books grandma got me, and I buy and sell stocks. So that's math, and it's a lot more practical."

Her dad tilted his head and chewed thoughtfully, but her mother gave them both a look like they were crazy. So much for that argument.

"It's *math*," Mrs. Sachs said, "but it's not the math you're supposed to be learning in school. It's not the math you'll be tested on at the end of the year."

"Unless you're taking the Series 7," her dad said.

"What's that?" Lindy asked.

"Stock broker's exam."

"Stock brokers have to take exams?" Tracy said. "You mean tests don't end when you start real life?"

Mrs. Sachs cleared her throat. "Let's get back to the story here. I talked to the principal, and she had a chance to check in with all your teachers. She says you seem to be keeping up with most subjects fairly well, but math is going to be a problem. Since you've missed so much class, they think it'd be a good idea for you to switch from the advanced class to regular."

Lindy dropped her silverware. Hadn't she wanted her parents to acknowledge that she was hopeless at math? So why did it feel so lousy now that they did? Maybe because that meant Steph and Howe would have math together, without her, and she was already sure to be left out after being home for so long. She picked up her fork and began pushing rice around her plate. "I told you I'm stupid at math," she said.

"You're not stupid," her mom said. "You've just missed a lot of class. She also suggested you get a tutor to make sure you're up-to-date."

Lindy put her fork down again. This was even worse than moving down a track. "A tutor? Oh no. Please don't let it be David Wright." David Wright was president of the seventh-grade honor society, and he was constantly talking about how "rewarding" it was to tutor the kids in regular classes.

"David Wright?" said Mrs. Sachs. "I don't think that's his name. . . ."

"Is he short? Blond hair? Squeaky voice?"

Tracy laughed. "That must be Tom Wright's brother! That's the perfect description of him."

"No, this is a professional tutor," said Mrs. Sachs. "He teaches math at another middle school. Let me get his name." She got up and started looking around the pile of papers near the phone.

"I have to go to another school?" Lindy asked.

"No," said her dad. "He'll come here. For an hour a night to start, but then maybe switch to two or three times a week once you're caught up."

Mrs. Sachs opened a few pieces of folded paper, then she held one up. "Here it is. Mr. Margolis. Seventh-grade math teacher. Sunday at seven o'clock."

"Sunday night?" said Lindy. "He's coming here? But I might still be sick."

"Don't share any saliva with him," said Tracy, raising her eyebrows a couple times.

"I know *you* won't," said Lindy with a smirk, and Tracy's smiled faded.

Chapter 11
Financial Advisor

Mr. Margolis was short but sturdy. His head was shaved bare, but his eyebrows were thick and dark, and when he talked they jumped up and down on his forehead like excited black caterpillars. Even though they'd only just met, Lindy quickly realized that his eyebrows gave away his emotions, which gave away how she was doing. When she answered a question correctly, his eyebrows would arch up, stretching with happiness. When she did a problem wrong, his eyebrows would curl toward each other, like they were conferring on how to better explain things. When they got to graphing, which Lindy was disappointed to see she'd have to do even in the regular class, his eyebrows moved permanently closer together.

Mr. Margolis looked at his watch. "Why don't we call

it a night for tonight," he said. "Tomorrow we'll start with graphing."

Lindy pressed her palms into her eyes. "I can tell you now that I'm going to have issues. I just don't get the point of graphs."

Mr. Margolis raised just one eyebrow. "Graphs have a ton of uses. They're a lot more useful than some of this other math."

"Like what?" said Lindy.

"Graphs are the basis for calculus, for instance," he said as he stacked his books and opened his backpack.

Yeah, Lindy thought. *Real practical.*

Mr. Margolis tried again. "Graphs show change over time. So you can use them to predict the future. I used graphs all the time when I worked on Wall Street."

Lindy peeked through her fingers. "You were a stock trader?"

Mr. Margolis zipped up his backpack and put on his coat. "Yep, in my previous life."

"What kind of trading did you do?" Lindy asked, dropping her hands and sitting up straight.

"Stocks, mostly. But I started in bonds, and I experimented with futures a bit before I left."

"Why'd you leave?"

"Well, for a while it was a real rush," he said. "Exciting stuff, making lots of money. But it was a ton of work. It wore me out. And then I was almost forty, and I felt like there were more important things I could be doing than helping myself and a big company make money."

"Like teaching math?"

Mr. Margolis laughed. "Like teaching math. And I'll tell you, it's a lot more of a challenge than trading stocks."

"Really?" Lindy asked. "But the stock market changes so quickly. You never know what it will do."

Mr. Margolis's eyebrows seemed to smile. "The market's nothing compared to middle schoolers."

Lindy laughed.

"All right, I'm out." Mr. Margolis held out his hand for a fist bump. "Nice meeting you, Lindy. Get some rest. You might have to start school again soon."

"You really used to be a stock trader?"

"Seventeen years," said Mr. Margolis, and his eyebrows confirmed it.

Lindy returned his fist bump. "See you tomorrow."

Chapter 12

Healthy Return

Mr. Margolis was right about one thing: Graphs were all over the place in stock trading. There was a whole section—five chapters—on different charts and graphs in *Buying Stock for Dummies*. After he left, Lindy began poking around the online trading site, and she found pages of graphs, each one with a dizzying splotch of colored lines going every which way, like the finger paintings Lindy used to make in pre-school. If these graphs could somehow predict the future, like Mr. Margolis said, and tell her what the stock was going to do, Lindy wanted to know how. That'd be better than any magazine quiz.

When Mr. Margolis sat down at the dining room table Monday night, Lindy placed a printout of one of the more complicated graphs on the table. "Can you explain this to me?" she asked. She watched his eyebrows as he took it in.

"Whose portfolio is this?" he asked slowly.

"Mine," said Lindy. "I've got a hundred dollars to trade online while I'm sick."

"And you printed out this graph?"

"From the trading site."

"And you want to know how to read it?"

"Yeah. I want to know what all these lines mean and how they predict the future, like you said."

"Well, then," said Mr. Margolis, rubbing his hands together. "We've got to start at the beginning."

Lindy paid close attention as he explained about the x-axis and the y-axis and how one affects the other. This same information would have left her with a blank stare in math class, but put into stock terms, it made total sense. And Mr. Margolis was just as excited as Lindy. His eyebrows danced wildly when he started talking about stocks. Even though he claimed to love teaching middle school math, Lindy had a feeling he missed his old life.

"You only bought your shares recently," Mr. Margolis said toward the end of the hour, "but these stocks have been around a long time. You could take all the historical data about a stock's price and put it on a graph. Then you could see if it's been generally increasing or generally decreasing."

Stock or no stock, and mono or no mono, the thought of all that graphing made Lindy tired. "That would take a long time."

"It would if you had to do it by hand, but luckily there are computer programs that graph it for you. There's probably charting software on the trading website you use."

Lindy sighed. What was the point of learning all this math when computer programs could just do it for you?

Lindy spent Tuesday morning reading about charts in her stock book, then looking up charts of all her stocks online. Mr. Margolis was right; there was historical data on the website; she just had to look for it. The better she got at reading the charts, the more she realized just how useful they were. There were so many different types of charts to learn—line charts, bar charts, candlestick charts—that she spent all day working on that. She was so absorbed that she didn't even fall asleep once.

Even stranger, she didn't make a single trade until after two p.m. It was only when she closed the dozens of windows with charts that she even saw her accounts page.

"Whoa," Lindy said with her eyes wide. Her portfolio was now worth $188. It had gone up forty dollars since the market opened, without her making one trade. "I almost doubled my money," she said quietly. "In one week."

This made her feel better about the fact that she'd probably have to go back to school soon. It was possible to make lots of money even if she was in class most of the time that the market was open.

The cautious part of her—the part that held her back from eating Howe's cupcake at lunch—told her that maybe she should stop now before she lost it all. Cash out. Take the money and never look back.

But how could she not look back? She'd only just discovered the key to predicting stock performance. If she was good at this before, she was going to be *great* at this now. Cash out? No, what she needed to do was invest more. Make it bigger! If she could turn a $100 into $188 in one week, she could turn $188 into $400 in another. And then double that . . . and double that . . .

Her dreams were interrupted by a car honking right outside. Lindy looked from her portfolio to the time: two fifteen. Her doctor's appointment was at two thirty, and the honk must have been her mom, who had left work early to take her. Lindy grabbed her coat and ran outside.

"The bad news," Dr. Gupta said, after examining Lindy, "is that there's no way to tell if your mono is still contagious.

But the good news," she continued, "is that the swelling in your lymph nodes and spleen seems to have subsided."

"What does that mean?" Lindy asked.

"It means you're clear to go to school as soon as you feel up to it. Just take it easy if you're tired, and don't share any food or drinks for another month or two. You don't want to spread this to any friends."

"She can go to school tomorrow?" Lindy's mother asked.

"She can go this afternoon, if she'd like to," Dr. Gupta said.

Lindy looked at the clock. "School ended twenty minutes ago," she said.

"Too bad," Dr. Gupta said with a smile. "I bet you're itching to get out of the house."

Now that the doctor said it, Lindy did feel itchy. She could barely sit still on the whole drive home, and the minute she walked in the door she knew there was no way she could stay there until bedtime. She was ready to get back to her life. "Can I go to the Sweet Escape?" she asked.

"Sure, honey," her mom said. "Have fun. I'll see you at dinner."

Lindy galloped into her room and changed into a sweater and jeans. It was the first time she'd put on anything but sweatpants since she'd gotten sick, and the denim felt rough and stiff on her legs. She redid her ponytail and even brushed her teeth, grinning like crazy into the mirror. Howe would be at the Sweet Escape for sure, and now that he and Steph were friends, Lindy had a feeling Steph would be there too. She could just picture the way they'd jump up when they saw her, give her a big hug, and make room for her in their booth. She would even buy them all cookies, or maybe even one of those big fancy cakes, since she was on her way to becoming a millionaire.

The cold air felt fresh and invigorating. Never mind that her body had hardly moved in weeks. Never mind that her breath became short and her muscles ached from lack of practice. Never mind. She was going to see her friends, and she practically ran the whole way there.

Chapter 13

Adjusted Rate of Return

The windows of the Sweet Escape were frosted, but Lindy could make out the figures of Steph and Howe in a booth by the front. Without waiting to catch her breath, she opened the door and stepped inside, figuring they'd turn and see her when the bell chimed.

But she just stood there, grinning stupidly. Steph and Howe were there all right, but they didn't turn to the door. They were sitting opposite each other, both hunched over the table, their heads almost touching. They were both laughing.

Lindy walked up to their booth. "Hey!" she said.

They pulled their heads apart and looked up.

"Melinda!" said Steph. "Hi!"

Lindy grinned. "Hey!" she said again, still panting. "I'm back!"

"Cool," said Howe.

"Are you sure you're not still sick?" said Steph. "You sound kind of . . . tired."

"That's because I ran here. I couldn't wait to see you guys!"

"Hi," said Howe. He smiled, and Lindy saw that his braces were now blue. They'd been plain gray since he got them last year.

Lindy laughed and looked at the table. "Whose phone is that?"

"Mine!" said Steph. "Ahhh!" she sang, holding the phone up as though she were receiving it from heaven. "I got a smartphone, *finally*. My parents took me to get it last weekend."

"I'm so jealous," Lindy said. "Now I'm the only person in the whole seventh grade without a cell phone."

"You just might be," said Steph. "Even Howard has his old dinosaur phone."

"Hey, don't insult Dino," Howe said, taking out his flip phone and placing it on the table.

Steph giggled, but Lindy just stood there, waiting for Howe to add to not call him Howard. When he didn't, Lindy said, "Can I sit down?"

"Oh yeah!" said Steph. "Scooch down, Howard."

Howe scooched, and by the time Lindy had finished taking off her coat, Steph had stood up and slid next to him

ELISSA BRENT WEISSMAN

on the booth. *I guess they're just being cautious in case I'm still contagious,* Lindy thought.

"Hey, Lindy," said Steph. "can you pass me my coat and stuff?"

"Um, sure." Lindy sat down on the empty side of the booth and handed Steph's things over the table.

Steph piled her outerwear next to her, so that Howe had to move closer to the wall, and Steph closer to him. Howe turned pink, but Steph seemed content.

Lindy said, "So, what's up, guys? I'm coming back to school tomorrow. Fill me in!" She tried to think of some gossip Steph had told her online that she could ask about. "Cassie got glasses, right?" she remembered. "What do they look like?"

Howe fidgeted with the strings from his hood, and Steph looked off in the distance, as though she was trying to pull up a distant memory. "Oh yeah," she said. "I think they're kind of small, plastic."

"What color?" Lindy asked.

"I don't know. That was so long ago; no one really cares anymore. Now everyone's talking about cats wearing jump-suits."

Howe started laughing, and Steph laughed so hard, she fell onto his shoulder.

Lindy pretended she didn't see that. "Cats wearing jump-suits?"

Steph shook her head. "Sorry, inside joke."

"You'd like it, Lindy," said Howe. "In science we had to draw these diagrams of dissected frogs, but Steph's drawing was so bad that it looked like a cat wearing a jumpsuit."

Lindy wanted to laugh, but she just couldn't picture it. She wondered if this was why Howe used to leave whenever Steph arrived, because she and Steph usually talked about stuff he didn't care about. And Steph had always complained that Lindy and Howe had so many inside jokes, it was like they were speaking a foreign language. "I guess you had to be there," she said.

"Yeah," said Steph. "It was really funny, though."

"It sounds like it. Hey," Lindy said, brightening, "do you guys want some cookies? I can pay. I've been trading stocks online, and I've made a lot of money."

"Trading stocks?" Howe asked.

"Yeah," said Lindy. "It's kind of hard to figure out at first, but once you get the hang of it, it's totally addicting. You buy stuff and sell it, and the price of everything changes constantly, so you want to find stocks that are going to go up so you can buy shares when the price is low and sell them when the price is high."

Her friends didn't seem nearly as intrigued as they should

be. *I must not be explaining it very well,* Lindy thought. She knew what would do it. "I started with a hundred bucks," she said. "And now I have almost two hundred."

"No kidding," Steph said. "So what are you going to buy with the two hundred?"

"Well, cookies for you guys," she said with a smile. "And more stock. I'll keep trading to make more money."

Steph wrinkled her nose. "I'd buy front row tickets to a concert—any concert. I just *really* want to go to one. My parents said they'd buy me tickets for my birthday, but I don't really want to wait that long. What would you buy, Howard?"

Howe didn't even have to think. "A better processor for my laptop."

"You should buy a skateboard," Steph said to Howe. "I could see you skateboarding."

"What?" said Lindy. "No way."

Howe shrugged. "Maybe."

"I'd also buy a cute outfit to wear to the concert," Steph continued, "in case the band saw me in the front row and invited me backstage." She looked at Howe and giggled. "And I'd buy a cat in a jumpsuit."

Lindy wanted to stop the conversation from going back to cats in jumpsuits. "Well, right now I can buy us all cookies. Or one of those big cakes!"

"No, thanks," said Steph, standing and starting to put on her many layers. "I should get home, actually. I need to do my homework before ice-skating tonight. You'd *love* ice-skating, Lindy. It is *so* much fun."

Lindy's slumped back in the booth. "I can do the next session. Maybe I should use my trading money to pay for private lessons so I can catch up and be in your class."

"Yeah!" said Steph. "That sounds better than just buying more sticks."

"Stocks."

"Whatever."

Howe snickered, and Steph punched him jokingly in the arm.

"Do you want a cupcake, Howe?" Lindy asked.

"Nah," Howe said. "I need to go help my dad."

Lindy tried not to show her disappointment. "Yeah, I should probably get back home, anyway. The stock market closes at four, and I might need to make some last-minute trades. But I'll see you guys tomorrow in school."

"Yes!" Steph squealed. "I can't wait!" She put her messenger bag over the body and waved good-bye with both hands. The door chimed as she left.

Howe's dad called him from the counter. "Welcome back," Howe said to Lindy. "See you tomorrow."

"Thanks," she said. "See you."

Howe slid out of the booth, walked behind the counter, and then disappeared through the door to the back.

Lindy sat by herself and looked at the case of sweets. None of them looked as appealing as they had when she'd entered.

She walked home slowly. It was exhausting, and not just because her body was out of practice. Was there something weird about the way Steph and Howe were acting, or was it just that she wasn't used to them being friends? *I've been home for almost a whole month,* she reminded herself. *The dynamic is going to be different now that Steph and Howe are getting along. Once I'm back in school and we see each other every day, things will go back to normal.*

As hopeful as she was, she was still happy to get home and log in to her trading account, where she was on familiar ground and where she'd made thirteen dollars in the time she was gone. She thought about the way Steph and Howe huddled together over Steph's phone and laughed about cats in jumpsuits, making her feel like she was a visitor from another planet. It had only been four weeks, but what if everything about school tomorrow was just as strange?

Maybe Mr. Margolis was right; the stock market wasn't nearly as unpredictable as middle schoolers.

PART TWO

PART TWO

Chapter 14

Return

Walking into school and climbing the stairs to the seventh grade lockers, Lindy was relieved to see that everything was exactly as she'd left it. The pale green walls, the student-painted murals from fifteen years ago, the groups of kids clustered around lockers and outside homerooms.

"Lindy! You're back!"

Lindy turned from her open locker to find Cassie leaning against the panel of lockers next to her. Her reddish-brown hair was shorter than Lindy remembered, and it looked lighter now that she wore black plastic glasses. "Hey! I like your glasses."

Cassie's hand went up to the frames. She wrinkled her nose. "Thanks. I'm still not a hundred percent sure I like them, but I guess it's worth it to be able to see."

"Was the whole world fuzzy before?" Lindy asked.

"Totally!" said Cassie, smiling widely. "I didn't even realize it. But once I got these glasses and put them on, I just couldn't believe the difference. I had no idea how much I was missing!"

There was another thing Lindy had forgotten: how much she liked Cassie. Or maybe she hadn't realized it before because she'd spent almost all her time with Steph or Howe. "I think I'll probably feel that way today," Lindy said. "I've been home for so long, I have no idea what's going on at school."

"I don't think you really missed much," Cassie said. "But if you need help with any homework or anything, just let me know. Unless it's math. I'm in regular, and I'm still totally lost."

"You're in regular?" Lindy said. "I'm in regular now too. I'm supposed to get my new schedule in homeroom."

"Cool!" Cassie said. "It's not that bad. Maybe we'll have other classes together."

"Oh," Lindy said. It hadn't occurred to her that moving down a track in math might affect the rest of her classes. But when she got her new schedule in homeroom, she saw that it changed everything. Her new math class met sixth period, when she used to have lunch. Now she'd have lunch fifth period, without Howe or Steph or anyone else at her usual table. Who would she sit with? And how many more inside jokes would Steph and Howe share without her there? How were things supposed to get back to normal if she didn't even *see* her friends during the day?

And if being in all new classes wasn't hard enough, this was the first day Lindy was away from her trading account. She'd woken up early and put in some limit orders so that the computer would automatically make trades if some of her stocks hit a certain price, but not knowing what was going on—with the market or her classes—made her fingers itch for the keyboard.

By third period, chorus, she couldn't wait any longer. She asked to go to the bathroom, but instead she went to the library. Lindy was able to log in and make sure her account wasn't wildly off course before the librarian even looked away from the books she was shelving. She was going to go to the bathroom on her way back to chorus, just so that she wouldn't have technically lied to her teacher, but she figured it was better to get back quickly. Her heart was pounding as she walked back into the room, but she slipped back into the group without anyone even looking at her twice. That was easy, she realized as she joined in the song.

Rather than go into the cafeteria fifth period and risk

sitting alone, Lindy scarfed down her sandwich by her locker, then spent the entire period in the computer lab, making trades. She only made five dollars, but the time flew by so quickly that she was startled when the bell rang.

Lindy didn't know anyone but Cassie in her new math class, but she did know the answer to most of the graphing problems they did, thanks to trading. She couldn't wait to tell Mr. Margolis—and her mom. She also couldn't wait to look at her portfolio again, but her next class was gym, and there was no way she could sneak out to the library like she had during chorus, since the gym had its own bathroom.

When Lindy went into the locker room to change into her shorts, she saw Steph for the first time all day. Before her schedule change, gym was one of the only classes they didn't have together. Now it looked it'd be the only one they did.

Steph was saying to another girl, "I'm going to go this weekend!"

Lindy snuck up behind Steph and threw her arms around her.

Steph gasped and spun around, then hugged Lindy back. "Where have you *been* all my life!" she said. "You said you were coming back today, but then you weren't in any classes this morning, and you weren't at lunch."

"I know," Lindy said. "I had to move down to regular math, and it messed up my whole schedule."

Steph's mouth fell open. "We don't have any classes together anymore?"

"Well," Lindy said, "I think we have gym together."

"Right now? You have gym now, now?"

They both laughed.

"Yeah," Lindy said.

"Yes! I have to text Howard. We thought you were still sick." Steph took her phone from her gym locker and started typing on it. Lindy watched her, wondering if Steph having a phone meant she'd always manage to be the one left out even when she was right there and Howe wasn't. But then it dawned on her that it also meant she could trade stock without having to sneak off to a computer.

"Hey!" Lindy said. "Can I borrow your phone?"

"Sure," said Steph slowly, finishing up her text and sending it. "I know what it's like to not have a phone, so I will always share mine with you."

"Thank you," Lindy said. She took it and asked Steph to show her how to pull up a webpage. "Want to see my trading portfolio? I was up five bucks by third period today."

"You're still doing that?" Steph said. "Wait!" She put her hand on Lindy's. "I know what you can spend your money on. A bunch of girls from ice-skating are going to a Seth Carson concert next month, and tickets are a hundred bucks, but I asked my parents, and they said I could go! And get this: We're going all by ourselves—no parents. You should come!"

"I don't know if my parents will let me," Lindy said. Actually she did know: The answer would be no. She could hear all their reasons now: She was only twelve; she was still recovering from mono; it cost a hundred dollars.

The gym teacher shouted into the locker room, and Lindy and Steph realized they were the only ones left. Steph grabbed her phone and put it back in her locker, and the two of them ran out to the gym.

"What if you bought the ticket yourself?" Steph asked a few minutes later, when they were bumping and setting a volleyball back and forth. "With the money you made from your stock whatever-you-call-it?"

"Trading," Lindy said for what felt like the millionth time. "I don't know. I can ask." Even if her parents magically said yes, she didn't know if she wanted to spend her trading money on a ticket to a Seth Carson concert with some girls she didn't know. That would cut her account by more than half, and she was already so limited in which stocks she could buy because she had so little money to work with. She needed *more* cash in her account, not less.

"Or, if your parents say yes," Steph continued, "they can buy you the ticket, and you can spend your stock money on a cute outfit to go in. I'm going to go to the mall this weekend to buy something."

"Maybe," Lindy said. She missed the ball and walked back to get it, trying to think of a way to change the subject. "So, you and Howe are friends now." She tossed the ball casually over to Steph.

"Yeah, I guess you could say that."

"You guess? What do you mean?"

"I don't know." Steph's cheeks turned pink, and she missed the ball. "I mean, yeah," she said, after she retrieved it. "We're friends. He's actually really cool."

"I told you! You should have believed me. I have good taste in friends." Lindy set the ball high into the air.

"Well, obviously," Steph said with a grin. She caught the ball and held it. "Oh my gosh, he said the cutest thing today at lunch."

"*Howe* did?" Lindy asked. *Cutest?* she thought. Howe said smart things and funny things—off-the-wall things, sometimes, even—but cute things?

"Mm-hmm. He had a cupcake that his dad made, and the frosting was kind of smushed in on both sides, and he was like 'My cupcake has a Mohawk.'"

"I said that!" Lindy blurted out.

Steph raised one eyebrow and tossed the ball to Lindy. "Um. Howe said it. You weren't there."

The ball flew over Lindy's head, and she didn't bother trying to get it. "Not today, obviously. But I said that, like, a month ago when he had a Mohawk cupcake. His cupcakes always get smushed, so we started calling them Mohawk cupcakes. You never heard us say that before?"

Steph shook her head.

"He didn't say that that's what we—like me and him—call it? He just said it like he was saying it for the first time?" Lindy knew she was probably making a big deal out of nothing, but it didn't feel like nothing. It felt like a kick in the ribs.

Steph shrugged. "Maybe he did say you guys say it. I don't remember."

"Whatever," Lindy grumbled, looking around the gym. "Where did our ball even go?" She found it at the far corner of the gym, and she got hit in the head with another ball on her way to get it. She threw it to Steph from far away—too far to bother trying to talk. The two of them stayed at that distance, silently setting the ball back and forth, until it was time to get changed.

Chapter 15
Liquid Surplus

By the time Lindy got home, her anger about the cupcake had mostly worn off. So what if Howe had reused her joke with Steph and passed it off as his own? It was hard trying to get things back to normal, and it was only going to be harder if she and Steph fought over little things. She decided that she want to go to the Seth Carson concert. It would be fun, and it would put her and Steph back on the right track.

Even though she knew she might get a better response from her mom if she asked in person, Lindy couldn't wait. She called her mother's work number as soon as she'd put down her backpack and taken off her coat.

"Well," said her mom, "how was it?"

"How was what?" Lindy asked.

"Your first day back at school!"

"Oh, it was fine. Steph and some girls from ice-skating are going to a Seth Carson concert, and she asked if I could go. Can I go? Please?"

"Oh, I don't know, Melinda," her mom said. "You should probably take it easy for a little longer. I don't think it's a great idea for you to go to a concert."

"But it's not till next month, and Steph's going," Lindy said. "It's Steph's first concert, and it would be my first concert, and we want to go to our first concert together."

Lindy's mom sighed. "Can we talk about this when I get home? How much does it cost?"

Lindy tried to be casual. "Tickets are a hundred bucks."

"What!"

"I know it's a lot, but it's Seth Carson, Mom."

"A hundred dollars? And I'd have to buy one for myself, too. That's two hundred dollars for a concert that you probably shouldn't be going to anyway."

"You don't need to buy one," Lindy said. She could feel this conversation combusting even as she said it, but she couldn't help from lighting the fuse. "Nobody's parents are going." When her mom didn't say anything for a few seconds, Lindy added hopefully, "So it's only one hundred."

Her mother said something to someone at work before coming back to the phone. "Lindy, I'm glad your first day back was fine, and I'm glad you're feeling well enough to think about going to a concert. But you're only twelve, and that's too young to go by yourself. Heck, it's too young to go to *anything* that costs a hundred bucks a ticket."

"But, Mom——"

"I have to go, Melinda. We can talk about this when I get home. But I don't think my answer is going to change."

Lindy kept her good-bye calm, then threw the phone down with a scream. It was all so unfair. *Nothing* was going her way. She was losing her friends, and her parents wouldn't let her do anything fun, and she couldn't even keep up with the one thing she was good at—day-trading—because she had to be in stupid school all stupid day.

She stomped into her room, yanked open the laptop, and pounded her fingers onto the keyboard to bring up her portfolio. The way this day was going, she'd probably lost all her money since third period.

But what she saw made her freeze. She hadn't lost all her money; she'd made even more. Her portfolio was now worth more than two hundred dollars. She still had an hour until the stock market closed for the day; with some well-placed trades, she could raise that even higher. Maybe Steph was right and her mom would let her go to the concert if she bought her own ticket.

Her eyes moved down from her portfolio to her parents'. She hadn't even looked at her dad's stocks since she started trading her own. But now she clicked on his account, just curious to see if her parents had a hundred bucks to spare.

The two stocks Lindy had bought for him were still there, and they were still up, though they hadn't been rising as dramatically as they had initially. A couple other stocks were there too, with a few shares, plus something listed as a mutual fund—Lindy was pretty sure she'd skipped that section of the stock book because it said mutual funds are slow-moving, long-term investments, and she wasn't interested in that.

What caught her eye was the line that said, "capital." That was the money that was in the account but wasn't invested in any stock. It was money that was just sitting there, not doing anything. Lindy's portfolio had zero capital; all her $213 was in stocks.

But her parents had a lot of capital. A ton. A dizzying amount.

"We're rich," Lindy said with a small breath.

She felt her anger returning. She knew her family wasn't poor, but she had no idea they were rich. Why were they letting all this money sit in reserve capital? Lindy wondered. They could be turning it into more money. Doubling her hundred dollars was a lot, but doubling *this* amount—now that would be incredible.

"What's up, Lind?"

Lindy jumped up, hitting her knee on her desk and spilling a cup of water that had been sitting there for at least a few days. "Geez, Tracy," she said, grabbing a shirt from the floor and using it to sop up the water. "You scared me. I didn't even know you were home."

"I can see that. You were staring at the screen so hard, I thought you fell asleep with your eyes open. What are you looking at?"

Lindy quickly closed the window and shut the laptop. She remembered how strongly her dad had made her promise not to reveal what was in their portfolio to anyone. She didn't think Tracy counted as anyone, since she was a member of the family, but now that she knew just what was in there, she understood why it was private.

"Come on," Tracy said. "I won't tell anyone. What were you doing?"

"Nothing," Lindy assured her. It felt weird to know how much money her parents had. She wished she hadn't seen that number. That crazy, high, unfathomable number. She didn't want to know that her mom was lying when she said they couldn't spend a hundred dollars on a concert ticket—they could buy the entire concert hall! And she especially didn't want to think about how much crazier, higher, and more unfathomable it could become with some smart investing.

"I wasn't doing anything," she repeated.

This time, she was assuring herself.

Chapter 16
Analysis Paralysis

Lindy tried not to think about how much money her parents had, she really did. But it was like when someone said, "Don't think about gray elephants," and then all you could think about were gray elephants. The harder she tried to block it out of her mind, the more it just came barging into her brain like it lived there, sprawling across the sofa and making itself comfortable.

She didn't bother asking about the concert again just yet, because she knew she wouldn't be able to have the conversation without revealing what she knew. When her mom flipped through the circulars and tore out coupons to save twenty-five cents on orange juice, she thought, *But you could buy up all the orange trees in Florida!* When they sat down to a dinner of flounder, rice, and broccoli, she thought, *We could be eating lobster and filet mignon!* And when Steph went on about the clothes she was buying to wear to the concert, and Howe didn't want to hang out unless it meant playing his three new video games, Lindy thought, *Why don't my parents spend any of their money on* me?

She tried to replace thoughts of her parents' wealth with learning how to make her own. Every morning before school, she read news headlines to see if there was any big economic news that might affect the market that day. After she got home, she kept CNBC on the TV to keep up with the movement of the market. And during the day, she spent her lunches in the computer lab and did some quick checking on Steph's phone from the gym locker room.

The trading website her parents subscribed to wasn't the most advanced or precise, but in some ways that made the process more manageable; it prevented her from being overloaded with information. She couldn't see Nasdaq Level 2 price quotes or get time and sales prints, but she could place alerts and limit orders. She didn't have five monitors attached to her computer like Mr. Margolis used to (he'd even shown her a picture of his office, which was a sea of desks and screens), but she did figure out how to hook up the old desktop monitor to the laptop so that she could have two screens, one older, boxier, and fuzzier than the other.

If what her mother always told her wasn't right about math, it certainly was right about trading: When she put her mind to it, she could be successful. Lindy developed a strategy that worked. She was making money. *I'm good at this,* she thought.

If only she had more money to work with.

On Tuesday, Lindy had to go to the doctor at eleven o'clock for a follow-up visit. Her mom took her out to lunch after, and at that point it didn't make sense for her to go back to school, even though her mom had to go back to work. Home alone during prime trading hours, Lindy knew this was the perfect opportunity to make some serious cash. She tuned into CNBC and loaded the trading site. An analyst on TV mentioned a stock that sounded like a great buy, so Lindy pulled up a quote. $145. With her own money, she'd only be able to buy one share. She sighed and went back to the main accounts page, where she found her parents' capital staring back at her.

According to her stock book, active traders borrow money from their stockbrokers so they have more to invest. Mr. Margolis told her that his company traded with borrowed money all the time. "It's called margin," he told her. "It's short-term borrowing. You get a loan, hopefully use it to make a profit, and then return the loan and keep the profit." He said something about a loss, too, but that part wasn't as important.

Margin, she thought, imagining Mr. Margolis's explanatory eyebrows. *Short-term borrowing.* It could possibly be so short-term that the person you borrowed from wouldn't even need to know it. Like over the summer when she borrowed Tracy's jacket after Tracy left for the night, wore it to get an Italian ice with Steph, and had it back in her closet before she returned.

I could borrow just a little *bit from my parents,* Lindy thought. *They'd never even have to know.*

Chapter 17
Recognition Lag

The phone rang, forcing Lindy to pull her eyes from her parents' account.

"Hello?" said Lindy.

"Hey, hey!"

Lindy gave one last glance at her parents' capital before she closed the top of the laptop. "What's up, Steph?"

"I'm on my way home from school. Do you want me to bring you the homework for today?"

"Yeah," Lindy said. "I can get the math from Cassie, so I really just need social studies."

"I'll be there in two minutes," Steph said. "But I can't stick around. Nick forgot something at school, so my mom needs to take him back, and then she'll pick me up before she has to take the twins to karate."

"Jujitsu!" came a voice from near Steph.

"Whatever," said Steph. "Lindy doesn't care."

"But they're totally different," said a different but very similar voice.

Lindy could practically hear Steph fluttering her eyelids. "Anyway, Lindy, is it okay if I come hang out for ten minutes?"

"Of course," Lindy said. "You don't have to ask."

"Okay, see you in a minute and a half."

A minute and a half! Lindy looked around and realized that the living room was a mess. You could barely see the couch and coffee table beneath all her trading books and printed-out charts. She hadn't cleaned her room all week either. Normally she wouldn't think twice about making Steph carve out a place on the bed or floor between the aftermath of a monsoon, but this was the first time Steph was coming over in a long time, and Lindy didn't want to take any chances.

She scooped all her charts into a few sloppy piles and stuffed them into her trading books to mark the pages. She heard a car pull into the driveway, and she moved the laptop into her room, then started pushing a mound of clothes from the floor into the closet. It was a minor miracle that she was able to close the closet door. She hoped Steph wouldn't have any reason to open it—whoever touched that door was going to fall victim to a clothing avalanche.

ELISSA BRENT WEISSMAN

Lindy redid her ponytail in the mirror and powered off the TV just before the doorbell rang. "Hey!" she said, opening the door wide.

"Hello." Steph stepped inside and pushed back her hood. "My brothers are completely ridiculous." She pulled off her mittens and stuffed them into her coat pockets. "They spent the rest of the ride here explaining the differences between every form of martial arts known to man. Tae kwon do is from Korea," she said, impersonating Nick, "while karate is actually from Japan."

Lindy felt herself getting warmer inside. Maybe she had nothing to worry about. Things between them were perfectly fine. "Fascinating," she said with a smile.

"Tell me about it." Steph took off her messenger bag and plopped down on a chair. She took out her social studies binder and handed Lindy the homework.

"Can I have your notes, too?" Lindy asked. "I'll copy them and give them back tomorrow."

"Oh, sure. Why don't you just hang on to the whole binder. I don't need it for the homework. I'll just stop by your locker in the morning."

"Okay," Lindy said. "Thanks." She put the binder on the coffee table and sat down on the couch.

"So," said Steph. She started running her finger over the

arm of her chair. "Have you asked your mom about the concert yet?"

"I asked once and she said no," Lindy started.

"Oh," said Steph. "Oh well."

"But I'm going to ask again. I think she'll change her mind if I tell her I can buy my own ticket."

"Well," Steph said slowly, "if not, we'll go to another concert together soon."

"I think she'll say yes," Lindy said. "I just have to ask at the right time."

"Well," Steph said again, more upbeat this time, "I was thinking that maybe it'd be better if you didn't come to this one. I mean, we were talking about it at ice-skating last night, and I don't want you to come if you're going to feel left out. Since you don't really know any of these girls."

"I won't feel left out," Lindy said. "I'll have you."

"Yeah," Steph said. Now she met Lindy's eye. "But it's just, you know, I only *just* started becoming friends with these girls, and a lot of them are in eighth grade, and they don't really know you. We all have ice-skating in common, and we love Seth Carson, but you've just been busy with this stock stuff."

Lindy cocked her head.

"I'm sure they'd like you," Steph said quickly. "But they don't *know* you, you know? So it might be weird."

"Oh," Lindy said. The hurt of what Steph was saying was starting to seep in. "I get it."

A car honked outside, and both girls jumped up. Steph hung her bag over her shoulder and gave Lindy a hug. "I'll see you tomorrow. And once you're old enough to go to a concert, we'll go to one together, I promise!"

Chapter 18
Margin Emergency

Lindy stared through the glass door as Steph got into the car, her anger rising. Once she was *old enough* to go to a concert? "Last time I checked," she said aloud as she slammed the door, "we're both the same age." She walked back to the couch, her fists clenching. "Actually," she yelled to nobody, "I'm a month older than you, *Steph*. But what, I'm not cool enough to hang out with your new friends? You'd be embarrassed to bring little Lindy along to this oh-so-adult concert?" She grabbed Steph's binder and started whipping through the pages. "Are these notes from your college class, since you're so grown up? They're all in purple pen. How mature!"

She threw the binder back on to the coffee table, and the rings opened, spilling papers all over. "Grr!" She wasn't

even going to bother picking them up—*take that, Steph*—
but something in the margin caught her eye. All the class notes
were written with Steph's favorite purple pen, but this was in
black. And it wasn't Steph's handwriting. It was Howe's.

I like your shirt.

Her heart beginning to beat faster, Lindy grabbed that
page. Underneath Howe's comment was one in purple from
Steph, then another from Howe. A whole conversation in
the margin.

> Thx! I'm so bored!
>
> Me too. Are we going out this weekend?
>
> Going out or hanging out?
>
> I guess going out. If you want.
>
> OK! ☺
>
> OK cool.

Lindy looked up at the date on the notes. Yesterday. Her
two best friends—who practically hated each other until
Lindy got sick—were not only *dating*, but in the whole day
and a half that passed since it happened, neither of them
had even thought to tell her. Lindy had to restrain herself

from ripping the page into a million pieces. If she hadn't spent her lunch periods and afternoons focused on trading, and all her evenings with Mr. Margolis, she no doubt would have found out from someone else. But that didn't excuse Steph and Howe. Did they think she wasn't mature enough to know? What kind of friends were they?

A rustling outside meant Tracy or her mom was arriving home, and Lindy didn't want to see or talk to either of them. Tightly gripping the evidence, she stomped into her room—the room she'd rushed around cleaning for nothing, seeing as Steph spent her whole visit in the living room, telling Lindy she was a baby. Lindy kicked her closet door. All the clothes she'd stuffed in there came crashing out and settling around her. "GRR!" Lindy screamed, making her throat burn.

But then she saw the laptop on her desk. She climbed out from the clothing pit and logged in to the trading site. *They think my hobby is babyish?* she thought. Her portfolio was up three percent on the day. But three percent of two hundred was only six dollars. *I don't need friends,* Lindy thought. *What I need is more money.*

Her eyes went down a line to her parents' available capital, and the cursor followed. It was time to make the margin work for her.

Chapter 19
Calculated Risk

Every book she read said it: An active trader had to have an appetite for risk. The market could swing any way in any moment, and day traders had to accept that. You could earn lots of money one day and lose lots the next. That's what made day-trading so scary, but also so exciting, as long as the risk was not too large. Being successful meant calculating risk, developing a plan, sticking to it, and being ready for anything. For Lindy, this applied not only to her actual trading, but to sneaking to the library during school to check her portfolio, and most importantly, to making sure her parents didn't find out that she was now trading using their account.

So when Lindy's father asked if he could grab the laptop and log in to the trading account the next morning, Lindy's heart started beating faster, but she was ready.

"What do you need to do?" she asked, casually splitting open an English muffin with a fork.

"I just want to check our portfolio," her dad said.

"The computer's downloading some updates," Lindy said, "so you can't log in right now." She opened the toaster oven and laid her English muffin on the rack.

"I hate when it does that," her dad said, scratching his beard. "An English muffin sounds good, actually. Can you put one in for me, too?"

Lindy almost said something too agreeable, like *Of course, Father,* but she stopped herself. She had to sound normal. "Sure." She opened the package and split another.

"How long till it's done?"

"I don't know, Dad. It's an English muffin. Two minutes?"

"No, the computer. How long till it's done downloading?"

"Oh. Probably a while. But I can log in after school and call you at work."

"Eh, I'll just do it after work. I need to sell some things. . . ." He trailed off, moving his head back and forth as if he was saying, *You know how it is.*

"I can sell it for you. The market will be closed when you get home, anyway. What symbol and how many shares?"

"Nah, don't worry about it. I'll just do it later."

Lindy's mom called from down the hall.

"Yes?" Mr. Sachs called back.

Her voice came closer. "What are you doing?"

"Talking to my daughter."

Mrs. Sachs rushed into the kitchen, all dressed for work. "Talking about what? I thought I heard the words 'symbol' and 'shares.' Is Tracy up?"

"Tracy's in the bathroom," Lindy said. "She's been in there since I woke up. I haven't even gotten to brush my teeth yet."

"Tracy, Lindy needs to brush her teeth!" she called. "Now, what were you two talking about?"

"I think the English muffins are done," said Mr. Sachs.

"It's only been, like, thirty seconds, Dad," said Lindy.

But her dad went to the toaster anyway and opened the door. He pulled out one half, which was still soft and not nearly brown. "You're right, Lind. A little longer. But I'll get the butter ready."

"You're avoiding my question," Mrs. Sachs sang as she stuck a tea bag into her travel mug and then filled it with water. "Were you talking about stocks? It's okay if you were."

"We were," said Lindy.

"We were talking about Lindy's stocks," said her dad. "The portfolio she's built with that one hundred dollars we gave her."

"Not our stocks?" said her mom.

"Of course not," said her dad.

"Dad's lying," said Tracy, who swooped in, a towel wrapped around her head, and took a granola bar from the drawer.

"What?" said Lindy. "You don't even know what we're talking about."

"True," said Tracy. She ripped open the wrapper and took a bite. "But I don't need to. Dad's just that bad of a liar." She disappeared down the hall and into her room.

"I think she's right," said Mrs. Sachs. "Honey, you promised. We're going to get a professional."

"I know," said Mr. Sachs. "I wasn't going to do anything, just check. *Now* the English muffins are ready. You want butter, Lind?"

"You can check when we meet with a professional."

"Yes, butter," said Lindy. "What are you talking about? A professional?"

"We're talking about," said her mom, "me not being comfortable with your dad trading stocks by himself online. And how we agreed to not do any more trading until we consult with a professional."

"What about me?" Lindy asked.

"You can still do your thing," her dad said.

　　　　　ELISSA BRENT WEISSMAN

Permission granted, Lindy thought.

"But I can't." He pouted. Then he caught his wife looking at him and turned the pout into a fake smile. "I'm just kidding," he said. "You're right. We should consult a professional. I won't even log in to *look* at our portfolio until we figure that out."

"Thank you," said Mrs. Sachs. She gave him a kiss.

Lindy could hardly believe her luck. She hid her happiness and relief by taking a big bite of her English muffin. Now her dad wouldn't log in and see that she'd started trading on margin.

"You look happy," Lindy's mom said to her. She took her tea from the microwave and then dropped the tea bag into the trash.

"It's winter break next week," Lindy said.

"Yes, lots of time to hang out with your friends."

Lindy shrugged. "Lots of time to trade, since I won't be in school."

"Don't go too crazy with that," Mrs. Sachs said.

"Go crazy," Mr. Sachs said. "Make a fortune."

Lindy smiled. *Permission granted,* she thought again.

At school, Lindy leaned against her locker. She held Steph's binder (which she'd grudgingly put back together) with one hand and twirled her hair with the other. Steph was going to come by any minute to pick up her notes, and Lindy didn't know what to do. She could pretend she hadn't seen the conversation in the margin, or she could flat out ask Steph if she was going out with Howe. Both options had their risks, and neither seemed like it'd yield a big reward. Neither would turn back time and make their friendship what it used to be.

But it turned out Lindy didn't have to say anything. When Steph came by, Howe was with her, and they were holding hands.

"Hi, Lindy," Steph said.

"Hey," said Howe.

Lindy looked pointedly at their hands, then at their faces. Steph took a breath and smiled, but Howe turned red and looked down the hall.

"Can I have my binder?" Steph asked.

Lindy held it out, and Steph took it.

"See you in gym!" Steph said. She skipped off toward her homeroom, dragging Howe behind her like a shy puppy. He glanced back and gave Lindy a half wave, but she didn't return it.

ELISSA BRENT WEISSMAN

Chapter 20
Trending Upward

With Steph in La-La Love Land and Howe pretending Lindy didn't exist, Lindy had lots of time and energy to throw into trading, and it was paying off. Things were going stupendously. Lindy stuck with the strategy she'd developed for her own stock, only now she had more options because she had more money to play with. She limited herself to a certain amount of her parents' money at first, and she grew that amount by almost twelve percent in just a few days.

On the last day of school before winter break, Cassie asked her during math if she wanted to go to the mall that night. "We leave for vacation tomorrow morning," she said, "and I still don't have a Christmas present for my mom. Do you want to come?"

Lindy said yes without even having to think. She didn't

have any other plans, and her trading was going so well that she had money to spend. Cassie bought a scarf for her mom, and Lindy bought one for herself. They tried on glasses frames and party dresses, and they got a strip of silly pictures of themselves from a photo booth. Then they bought soft pretzels and walked around the food court trying every free sample twice. They had so much fun that Lindy didn't think about Steph or Howe once. "I wish you were going to be around during the break," Lindy said before Cassie's mom dropped her off that night.

"Yeah," Cassie said, "we'll have to hang out more next year."

"Next year? Like in eighth grade?"

"Well, yeah. But also next year as in January."

"Oh!" Lindy said, laughing. "Yes!"

The next morning, she logged into the trading site and saw that her parents' account was up even higher. Her parents were at work, her sister was still asleep, the charts were trending upward, and the day was hers. Brimming with confidence, she decided to let herself borrow just a little bit more from her parents. And boy did it pay off. By dinnertime, she'd made a whopping *two thousand* dollars— in one day! It was going to be a new year in just over a week, and it was going to be stupendous.

Chapter 21
Panic Buying

But then things started to get worse. Her mother had Monday off, so all the Sachs women went out to brunch. Lindy came home and found that her parents' portfolio was down six percent on the day, and it was only eleven thirty a.m. Without even taking off her coat, she checked the newspaper home page, which told her that the holiday shopping season had been much worse than expected for retailers, and a big bank had reported record losses. "Shoot," she said aloud. That sort of news could do anything to the stock market. She wondered if she should sell most of her stocks and not trade at all for a day or two. But then she heard her mother walking toward her room.

"Bad news?" asked her mother, who also had on her coat.

Lindy shut the laptop so her mother wouldn't peek at the screen. "My stocks are down."

"A lot?"

"For just a few hours, yeah."

"It can all change in one day," her mom said knowingly. "That's why I'm glad Dad isn't playing around right now. The more you risk, the more you can lose."

"Yeah," Lindy said, swallowing her guilt.

"Why don't we do something fun to take your mind off of that? We can go see a movie, or maybe we can check out some of those boutiques Tracy likes. They're starting to put out spring clothes already. Tracy has plans this afternoon, so I thought we could do something special, just me and you."

"That sounds great," Lindy said, hoping she sounded sincere. "Do you think I could just look at my portfolio for, like, a half hour before we go? The market is going crazy today."

"Oh okay." Her mother hovered at the door for a moment. Then she brightened. "Why don't you show me what you do here," she said with genuine enthusiasm. "You've gotten so into it, and I don't even know how to download the stock thingamabob."

Lindy could picture the screen that would pop up when she opened the computer. It would show, perfectly clearly— even to someone who thought you had to "download the stock thingamabob"—how much money she was trading with and how much money she'd lost this morning.

"Actually," Lindy said, "I don't think I need to check it. Let's go."

"Are you sure? I really am curious to see you do your stock thing."

"No," Lindy said. She stood up. "I can do that any day. Let's go see a movie, since you're home."

Mrs. Sachs smiled and put her pocketbook on her shoulder. "All right! Let's go!"

They caught a one p.m. movie and then went to a couple boutiques, so by the time they got back, the stock market was closed. And it was even worse than Lindy could have imagined. The market was so far down that almost all the money she made over the past week was gone. The lines on all her charts were in the shape of a rollercoaster—a slow, steady rise before a scream-inducing drop. *In one day!* Lindy thought angrily. She wondered if she should keep the tags on the clothes her mom had bought her.

All her favorite trading blogs and the articles in the business section of the newspaper confirmed that Lindy wasn't the only one who lost money. This was, officially, a terrible day for Wall Street. The market posted one of the biggest single-day drops in more than a year. Some experts thought it was the start of a long period of even greater losses. Others thought this was a freak reaction, and the market would rebound fairly quickly. She heard the news on TV talking about it while she brushed her teeth that night. When she finished, she went into the living room and sat on the arm of the couch. "What do you think, Dad?" she asked.

Mr. Sachs shrugged. "Who knows. I think it'll rebound to some degree."

"Now could be a good time to buy," Lindy said. "If it is going to go up. Buy low, sell high, right?"

"Yeah, but that's a lot easier if you know it's going to go up, which no one does. I'm just glad I listened to your mom last week and got out when I did."

He looked at Lindy, and she willed herself to think about happier things than what she'd done, in case her face gave away her thoughts. *Hanging out with Cassie, chocolate cake, having a pet monkey* . . .

"How'd you do today?" Mr. Sachs asked. "Take a beating?"

"Yeah," Lindy admitted.

He nodded and rubbed his beard. "Everyone did."

"I'll gain it back tomorrow, though."

"I hope you do."

You have no idea.

Chapter 22
Feeling Bullish

She didn't gain it back tomorrow, or the next day. As much as she tried to stop it, she lost even more. She spent New Year's Eve with her parents, watching the ball drop on TV and worrying about how much lower their portfolio was going to drop. The new year wasn't looking so promising after all.

Mr. Margolis came to tutor her the night of January first. "If you were still a stock trader," Lindy said to him, trying to sound casual, as if only one hundred dollars was at stake, "what would you do if the whole market keeps going down, like it has this past week?"

Her tutor's eyebrows wiggled in thought. "Depends. If I were a regular investor—you know, long-term—I'd probably ride it out. The market tends to go up in the long-term."

"But in the short-term?" Lindy asked. *If you have to get*

back money you lost that you borrowed without telling the people you borrowed it from?

"In the short-term, I'd probably try to hedge as best I could."

"Hedge?" Lindy asked. "Like hedges?" She thought of the hedges in her backyard, which grew so quickly in the summer that if her dad took one week off from trimming them they'd invade the neighbors' yards. What did hedges have to do with stocks?

"No, hedge your bets," Mr. Margolis explained. "That means to cover yourself, so you're not too exposed to risk. It means you don't want to bet on only one situation."

"But you're not betting," Lindy said. "You're trading."

"That's what trading is, though, right?" Mr. Margolis said with a shrug. "When you buy stock in a company, you're betting that that company will do well and you'll be able to sell the stock for a higher price later. Trading is nothing more than betting, really. There's a lot of strategy involved, but there's also a *lot* of luck."

Lindy slumped back in her chair. It didn't feel like she just had good luck when her stocks were all going up; it felt like she had a natural skill. But maybe that's all it was: luck. And now it was running out.

Focusing on the strategy part of it—bullishly sure she

could reverse the downward trend of her parents' portfolio—Lindy stayed up long after Mr. Margolis left, researching stocks that might move up, however little, the next day. She looked back through her trading history and checked the charts of stocks that had performed well. She skimmed countless investing websites and blogs. School started again on the third, and she'd be back to having only lunchtime and after school to trade. She wouldn't even be able to check her stocks during gym, seeing as she wasn't talking to Steph. That meant tomorrow was her last chance to make back this money.

It was nine o'clock, and the market opened in a half hour. Lindy had no time to lose. She turned on the TV to CNBC and pulled up the home page of the *Wall Street Journal*. She read through her notes from last night and reviewed the important charts. At 9:29, she had her order typed and her cursor over the enter button.

She could do this. She was ready.

Chapter 23
Fill or Kill

But the market wasn't ready to cooperate. Lindy's first order was for one thousand shares of a stock called NJNR. Her charts showed that NJNR had gained about one dollar every morning between nine thirty and ten a.m. for the past week. Lindy's plan was to buy a thousand shares right at nine thirty, then sell them twenty minutes later, hopefully for a dollar more, and make a quick thousand dollars. But at 9:35, NJNR had gone *down* from the price Lindy had bought it at.

"Don't panic," she told herself. She pulled up the line charts of NJNR's performance. The pattern she'd seen before was clear. Looking closer, she noticed that last Thursday, NJNR had dropped briefly in the first ten minutes, then had risen before ten o'clock. If it was doing that again—which

ELISSA BRENT WEISSMAN

it hopefully was—it meant Lindy shouldn't just wait for it to go back up, she should buy even more while it was lower.

So she put in an order for another five hundred shares. Then she waited with her knee shaking. She checked it every five seconds. And every five seconds it went down. Trying to be patient, she went to the kitchen and poured herself a bowl of cereal. But she was too nervous to eat, so after two spoonfuls, she left the cereal to get soggy and went back to the computer. NJNR had gone down even more. Now, instead of having gained a thousand dollars, she had lost almost a thousand. "If it goes down again the next time I refresh," Lindy swore, "I'll take the loss and sell." She counted to ten, then pressed refresh again.

"Yes!" she shouted. It had gone up! It was a slight movement, but it was a slight movement in the right direction. She refreshed again and stood up and danced around the room. It was up again! Confident it would continue to rise for at least another ten minutes, Lindy switched her focus to the next part of her plan.

This step involved a stock called FGY, which did so well for her that she already had five thousand shares in her portfolio. Her charts showed that even though FGY varied a lot throughout the day, it usually went up by about a dollar at some point. So now she bought another five thousand shares, and she placed a limit order so that the computer would automatically sell them all when the price went up by fifty cents. That should be a nice, safe bet, as Mr. Margolis would say.

When she finished setting up that order, she went to the kitchen, dumped out her soggy cereals and poured a new bowl. This time she ate the whole thing. She brushed her teeth—she hadn't done that yet—and changed out of her pajamas and into her lucky trading clothes: the sweats she'd been wearing the first day she started, when she made seventeen dollars. That day felt so long ago. Had she really been so excited about making seventeen dollars in one day? Could she really have lost only one hundred, max, back then? She wasn't just in a different ballpark now, she was playing a totally different game.

At 9:55, she checked on NJNR, which she was expecting to see up and ready to be sold for a profit. But it wasn't. It was down. *Way* down.

"No," Lindy said sharply. She refreshed. Down still. She refreshed the main page of her portfolio. Every one of her stocks was down. Not a single thing was up except for her heart rate.

By ten o'clock, NJNR was still going down. Lindy let it go another fifteen minutes, but it only went lower. She couldn't risk losing any more than this. So at 10:16, ready to cry, she sold all of her shares of NJNR. She'd lost almost two thousand dollars.

The day continued in the same fashion. A few of her quick transactions brought her small gains, but on the whole she continued to lose more . . . and more . . . and more and more and more. Looking for some assurance that she wasn't the only one doing badly, Lindy kept the TV tuned to business news. But it didn't give her the information she was hoping for. Instead of hearing that today was another day of record lows, she heard that the market was actually doing fairly well. That meant that not every stock was taking a dramatic plunge, just the ones Lindy was picking.

"I need to get all this money back," Lindy said, staring at the screen, "or my parents will kill me. And I'll deserve it." She was crying now, but her tears only blurred the image of the positions page, turning it into a sea of red, red, red.

"I've learned my lesson," she said through her tears. "I won't ever use money that isn't mine again, ever. I just need to get it back."

She suddenly remembered her last hope: FGY. She'd bought five thousand shares that morning, and the computer should have automatically sold them all by now, for a profit. That wouldn't wipe out all her losses, but it would help mitigate them, and it might help her feel slightly less miserable.

She wiped her eyes with her arm and took a big, sniffly breath. She clicked on FGY.

Lindy let out a slow, agonizing moan. It hadn't sold automatically—because it had never gone up. Her so-called safe bet had done nothing but sink and sink. She'd been so busy losing money on other stocks that she hadn't even checked it, or else she would have sold earlier and not lost as much. The charts were so solid, she hadn't even thought to have the computer automatically sell if it went *down*. But now she had to sell—she couldn't risk losing any more. She placed her last order of the day to sell all ten thousand shares. Instead of making a sure, easy, guaranteed $3,100, she'd lost an additional $5,600.

She didn't know what her parents would do when they found out. If they made her pay them back, she'd be working it off until she was fifty—probably even longer, since she wouldn't have a high-paying job; she'd lost all the money it would have cost for her to go to college. Maybe she should just run away and save them the cost of feeding and clothing her.

As terrified as she was to admit what she'd done, she needed to come clean to someone if she wanted to get advice.

Cassie was still away; her flight got in late that night. Even though she was still angry at Steph and Howe, she signed in to see if either of them could chat. But Steph had an away message up: spending my mom's money at the mall with my boy! :)

It made Lindy feel even sicker than she already did. Steph clearly wasn't going to be any help, and if "my boy" meant who she figured it meant, Howe wasn't going to be either. For them, spending their parents' money meant asking for twenty bucks to take to the mall. How could they really help Lindy get back the obscene amount of *her* parents' money she'd lost?

There was only one person—besides her parents themselves—who would truly understand the gravity of the situation, and who had as big a stake in the money as she did, whether she liked it or not. She was Lindy's only hope. And she was on the other side of the wall.

Chapter 24
Cushion Theory

"Tracy, I need some advice."

"You do, do you?" Tracy said grandly, though without looking up from the text message she was typing. "Which of my many areas of expertise do you need to call on, dearest Melinda?" She clicked her phone closed and placed it on her desk before looking up. "Oh my gosh, Lind. Have you been crying?"

Lindy shrugged, but then nodded. She felt a fresh tear come down her cheek, and she wiped it away with the back of her hand.

Tracy picked up a stack of clothes from her bed and moved them to the top of her dresser. "Come on, come in." Tracy climbed onto her bed and arranged her many pillows into two mounds against the headboard. Lindy's bed just

ELISSA BRENT WEISSMAN

had one pillow, for her head, but Tracy had almost a dozen, all different sizes and colors. Lindy often wondered how Tracy even found room to sleep with all those pillows. But now, as the two of them settled on side-by-side pillow piles, Lindy was glad for them.

"I did something really bad," Lindy said. "Mom and Dad are going to kill me if they find out."

"Well, maybe they don't have to find out," Tracy said, and Lindy was suddenly flooded with memories of how close she and her sister used to be and how much she missed that closeness. Tracy had been home all day, and the two of them hadn't even said hello.

"What did you do?" Tracy asked matter-of-factly. "Just tell me."

"It's really bad," Lindy repeated.

Tracy waited.

"I mean, really, really, *really* bad."

Tracy still waited in silence.

Lindy sighed. "Okay. You know how Mom and Dad gave me a hundred dollars to use to trade stocks when I was sick?"

"Yeah."

Lindy closed her eyes as she continued. "Well, at first I was just using that one hundred dollars, and I was doing really well." She kept her eyes closed as she went on, telling her sister about how she started trading in her parents' portfolio without letting them know, and how she was making money until the past few days, when she'd lost everything she'd earned and more. "I lost a lot of their money, Trace," she said, opening her eyes, looking at her sister, and trying not to cry. "A lot."

Tracy didn't say anything for a few seconds. Then she turned on her pillows and asked, "How much?"

Lindy gulped. This was the part she didn't want to say. But she knew she had to. "Twenty-five thousand dollars."

Chapter 25
Selling Short

Tracy's jaw dropped open in slow motion. It hung there, along with the air. The whole room seemed to be suspended.

"Twenty-five thousand dollars," Tracy repeated. "Like, two-five-zero-zero-*zero*. You're sure."

"I'm sure."

Tracy said a word under her breath that would have gotten her in trouble. But not in nearly as much trouble as Lindy was in.

"You have a lot of money saved . . . ," Lindy started.

"Yeah, like five hundred bucks, not twenty-five thousand!" Tracy's voice was starting to climb. "You know how long it would take to save twenty-five thousand dollars?"

"What about from your bat mitzvah?"

"Yeah, I got a lot from people at my bat mitzvah," Tracy

said, jumping out of bed and starting to pace the length of the room. Her pillows collapsed. "But it's all in my college fund—I can't touch it. And it's nowhere near twenty-five grand, anyway."

"What if we borrow it somewhere?" Lindy asked. "From the bank or something."

"What, just walk in and ask for it? Who's going to lend a fourteen-year-old and a twelve-year-old twenty-five thousand dollars?"

"I'll just tell Mom and Dad," Lindy said, resigned. "I'll work it off. And I'll pay them back all the money I get at my bat mitzvah."

"You're not going to have a bat mitzvah if Mom and Dad find out you lost twenty-five thousand dollars."

Lindy didn't know if Tracy meant she wouldn't have one because there'd be no money to throw her a party or because she wouldn't live to see thirteen.

"Jackie's sister is eighteen," Tracy said. "I can ask her to buy us a lotto ticket. That might be your only hope."

"Are you going to tell Mom and Dad?"

"No way," Tracy said. "But you're doomed when they find out. I don't think there's anything you can do."

Tracy sat down in her desk chair, still in shock, and Lindy started to cry again.

ELISSA BRENT WEISSMAN

"It'll be all right, Lind," said her sister. "You're not a bad person. It's not like you were *trying* to lose all that money. Everybody screws up. You just screwed up majorly."

Lindy looked at Tracy through her puffy, red eyes. She wasn't helping.

"You know who else screwed up majorly?" Tracy continued, shaking her head. "Dream Dry. Remember that blow-dryer I was telling you I wanted? Well, I'm so glad I don't have one now. Leigh Anne's mom was blow-drying her hair this morning, and it totally malfunctioned; she almost got electrocuted. She might sue the company."

Lindy sniffed. She'd forgotten about Dream Dry after that first day when she realized she didn't have enough money to invest in it, but now that Tracy mentioned it, she remembered seeing commercials for it on TV, promising a revolution in hair care. "This is the blow-dryer you said everyone is going to want?" she asked.

"*Was* going to want, yeah. Not anymore. They were making this really big deal about it coming out, and now they'll probably have to cancel the whole thing. They can't have their blow-dryers electrocuting people, obviously."

"Wait," said Lindy, the day-trader gears in her head starting to turn. "This just happened this morning? Was it in the news or something?"

"I don't think so," said Tracy. "I just heard about it from Leigh Anne."

"But once news comes out that Dream Dry can't sell this big new product, they're going to lose a lot of money, and people won't like them much anymore."

"*I* don't like them much anymore," said Tracy. "The Dream Dry 130-Z was going to change my life."

Lindy ignored that melodramatic claim and ran to her room to get the laptop and her copy of *Buying Stock for Dummies*. She could feel the blood starting to rush through her body, and her fingers started to tingle. "If I do this right," she said, "I'm pretty sure Dream Dry can get us our money back."

"Um, wouldn't it be the opposite?" Tracy asked, her voice suggesting that she knew how Lindy had lost so much to begin with. "I don't know much about stocks, but I'm pretty sure people who invested in Dream Dry are about to *lose* a lot of money."

"Exactly!" Lindy used the trading site to get a quote for Dream Dry. "Okay, here it is. DDRY. Fifty-one seventy-three." She clicked to pull up a chart showing its history over the past month. "It's been going up in general, including today. That means no one knows about the malfunctioning blow-dryer problem yet!"

"Lindy, don't be stupid," said Tracy. "That just means it hasn't gone down yet. Are you trying to lose another twenty-five grand?"

She has no faith in me, Lindy thought. *But wait till she sees this.* "What's it called . . . what's it called . . . ," she muttered, flipping through the *Buying Stock for Dummies* book.

"What are you looking for?"

"Found it!" Lindy read the definition to herself, then again out loud. "Short selling. Borrowing shares to sell at a high price, then buying those same shares low. If you short a stock"—she read this last part slowly and carefully, her smile growing with every word—"you make money when its price goes *down*."

Tracy's eyes widened as she took in the meaning of those words. "Serious?" she asked. "How does that work?"

"Let's say Steph really wants"—Lindy looked around the room and saw an old pair of Rollerblades in the corner of the open closet—"a pair of Rollerblades."

"Why?" said Tracy. "Rollerblades are so elementary school."

"Exactly. Let's say Steph doesn't know that, and she thinks they're cool. So I borrow your Rollerblades and sell them to her for twenty bucks."

"Okay . . . ," said Tracy.

"She uses them a couple times, and then she realizes that Rollerblades aren't really cool after all."

"Because they're not."

"So I say to her, 'I'll buy them back from you—for *ten* bucks.' Then I return the Rollerblades to you, and I keep the extra ten dollars."

"Because she gave you twenty," Tracy said slowly. "You sold them for a high price, and then you bought them back for a lower price, so you make money. You can do that with Dream Dry?"

"I've never done it before," Lindy said, "but it can't be too hard. I would basically have to borrow some shares from the trading website and sell them now, because the price is high. Once the news breaks, the price should go way down, and I'll buy those shares back, return the shares, and make money." She checked the time on the laptop: three forty-five p.m. She had fifteen minutes until the market closed, and if the news about the malfunction broke tonight, tomorrow morning could be too late.

Tracy watched as Lindy nervously searched through the help pages of the trading site to figure out how to borrow the shares and short the stock. The sound of the front door opening made them both freeze and look at each other.

ELISSA BRENT WEISSMAN

"It's Mom," said Tracy. "I'll distract her while you do this."

"Okay," said Lindy.

"Good luck."

"Thanks."

Lindy heard Tracy go into the living room and start saying, "What are your new years' resolutions, Mom?" Lindy almost laughed, but she had more important things to worry about.

By 3:57, Lindy had figured out how to put in a short order. She pulled up a real-time quote for DDRY, just to make sure it was still high. It was. Then she carefully typed in all the information into the order entry. If this worked, she'd have all of her parents' money back in their account once the news of the malfunction broke. If it didn't, the account would be down twice as much. But it was her best shot.

Just moments before the market closed for the day, Lindy crossed her fingers and pressed enter.

Chapter 26
Diner's Dilemma

Though it sometimes seemed to Lindy like she and her sister were from different universes, they did have a few things in common. One was that they were both painfully impatient—waiting for the market to reopen tomorrow to see what would happen with Dream Dry was just as excruciating for Tracy as it was for Lindy. Lindy knew because Tracy, like herself, took only a few bites of her dinner. That was another thing they had in common: Both sisters lost their appetites when they were nervous. And now they had a third thing in common: fear that their family might soon be broke.

"What's wrong, girls?" their mother asked. "Last time I made this chicken you both devoured it."

"And you always like my loaded mashed potatoes," added their father. "And tonight they're *extra* loaded."

"Extra loaded with what?" their mother asked, waiting for the answer with a forkful of loaded potatoes halfway between the plate and her mouth. "Butter?"

"And love," Mr. Sachs said.

Mrs. Sachs chuckled and rolled her eyes, but neither girl seemed to be paying attention.

"Are you girls feeling okay? You didn't catch Lindy's mono, Tracy, did you?"

"I'd better not have," said Tracy. She took a small bite of mashed potatoes.

"Are you feeling all right, Lind?" her mother asked.

Lindy looked at her plate and chewed slowly. This could be her chance. If she said she felt sick again, she could probably stay home a couple days and have more time to try to trade her way out of the pit she'd dug. But what if her stocks just kept plunging like they had the past few days and the pit only got deeper? She might as well be digging her own grave.

"I'm fine," Lindy said. She smiled, trying not to show that she was envisioning her own funeral.

Chapter 27
Rally

The first thing Lindy did in the morning was google Dream Dry to see if there'd been any breaking news about them overnight. Nothing. The first hit was the Dream Dry website, and its home page still had a fancy video describing the "revolutionary power" of the new Dream Dry 130-Z. No point in checking their stock price now. Until the bad news broke, there wasn't going to be any action, and she had to at least try to concentrate on school.

Her lunchtime visit to the computer lab showed that there was still no news. She sat in the computer lab, clicking aimlessly around the Internet until the bell rang. She threw her lunch in the trash on her way out.

Cassie gave her a big hug in math, and Lindy asked how her trip was.

"Are you okay?" Cassie asked.

Lindy didn't know how to answer that, so she considered herself lucky when their teacher told everyone to sit down and get ready to work.

To her surprise, Steph also gave her a big hug in the gym locker room. "Melinda!" she said. "I missed you so much over the break!"

Really? Lindy thought.

"And I have to tell you something important," Steph continued. "I think I'm in love."

Lindy didn't stop herself from rolling her eyes, though she did feel a little bad when she saw a flicker of hurt cross Steph's face. "With Howe?" she asked.

"Yes," Steph said. "No offense, but he's just so different when he's not around you. What we have is . . ." Steph's eyes searched the lockers for the right word. "Magical."

If they'd had this conversation a few days ago, Lindy would have had a lot to say, and most of it wouldn't have been nice. But today, she had more important things to worry about. "That's great," Lindy said. "Can I borrow your cell phone?"

Steph crossed her arms and stared at Lindy for a full five seconds, her eyes narrowing and her lips becoming tighter.

"Can I?" Lindy asked again. "It's really important."

Steph reached into her bag and held out her phone. Lindy took it, and Steph shook her head and walked away.

Lindy typed Tracy's number in the "send to" box. Then she wrote her message:

Trace its lind u hear anything?

She lingered in the locker room waiting for a response until her gym teacher opened the door and yelled for everyone to get outside. She tossed the phone in her locker before she ran out. She didn't make a single one of her basketball layups all period; her mind was on that phone and Tracy's response.

Back in the locker room, Lindy checked the phone before changing back into her jeans. Tracy had replied.

Yes!!! leigh anne's mom interviewed for news. on tonight. we might b ok!!!

Leigh Anne's mom was interviewed for the news. . . . That meant the story was breaking. And once the story broke, Dream Dry's stock *should* start to plummet. And once Dream Dry's stock plummeted, Lindy's portfolio would go back up. And once it went back up, she could sell everything and her parents would never know what had happened. And then she could give up day-trading forever.

"Can I have my phone back now?" Steph asked. She was back in her regular clothes, and her hair was down and freshly brushed.

"Yes," Lindy said. "Thanks."

"Whatever," said Steph. She took the phone and left.

Chapter 28
Up Volume

Both sisters came straight home from school. With Tracy over her shoulder, Lindy logged in to the trading site and saw that Dream Dry's stock had already dropped from $51.73, where Lindy shorted it, to $47.12.

"It went down," Lindy said. "Our position went up. It could be just an ordinary change for the day, but it seems like a big change for that."

"What does that mean?" Tracy asked.

"It means that it might have just gone down randomly, and it'll go back up. Or it could be the start of a big plunge."

"But so far," Tracy said, "we made money?"

"We made some."

"And if it plunges . . ."

"We'll make a lot."

Tracy rubbed her hands together. "Come on, plunge."

Their mother called to say she'd be home from work late, which suited Lindy and Tracy just fine. They spread their homework over the coffee table and turned on the television to wait for the news. Neither said much, but they were united in nervousness and angst, which made them feel like one.

Lindy was answering questions at the end of her science chapter when she heard the words she'd been waiting for.

"A local salon owner was in for a shock when she tried out a much-hyped new blow-dryer. We'll have the story at five o'clock."

Both girls' heads snapped up. Tracy started tapping her pen on her English binder. "That's it, that's it!" she said. "Go back, go back."

Lindy rewound and the commercial came on again, and this time they gave it their full attention.

"A local salon owner was in for a shock when she tried out a much-hyped new blow-dryer. We'll have the story at five o'clock." The newscaster's words were broadcast over silent footage of a woman standing in a salon, talking, and showing a blow-dryer to the camera.

"That's Leigh Anne's mom!" Tracy screamed. "And that's the Dream Dry 130-Z!"

"Five o'clock," Lindy said. She looked at the time. "It's only 4:15," she moaned.

"O, time!" Tracy said. "Why dost thou torture us so?"

Lindy looked at her with raised eyebrows.

Tracy shrugged and laughed. "Sorry," she said, pointing to her English binder. "Shakespeare unit."

Each minute felt stretched to capacity, but the five o'clock news did, eventually, come on. Tracy thanked god in Elizabethan English for having the story air within the first five minutes of the news. "My spirit and bladder canst not have waited another moment!" she cried.

"A local salon owner got the shock of her life when she agreed to test a new blow-dryer from Dream Dry," the news-caster said.

The scene cut to a clip from a Dream Dry commercial that said, "Get ready for a revolution in hair care."

"Turn it up!" Tracy yelled. Lindy fumbled with the remote, and Tracy grabbed it from her hands and made it loud enough for the whole block to hear.

"Dream Dry's newest product," the newscaster contin-ued, "the 130-Z, was scheduled to roll out next week, and the hairstyling industry was bracing for something big.

Dream Dry's patented new technology uses electrons to dry hair up to five times faster than an ordinary hair dryer, but also leave it feeling silky and virtually free of frizz. But Catherine Antonia, the owner of Salon Antonia in Midfield, was almost electrocuted by the device."

The scene cut to the salon, where Leigh Anne's mother was standing in front of a row of hair products, her own hair perfectly coiffed. "I got the 130-Z about two months ago—they gave prototypes to some salon owners to test it out and create some buzz. I was really impressed with it, until yesterday." She picked up a blow-dryer and showed it to the camera, holding it lightly between her fingers as though it might detonate. "I was blow-drying my hair, and it started to get really hot. My scalp was starting to burn, and the handle was heating up. I tried to turn it off, but it stayed on! So I dropped it onto the counter, and sparks began flying out of the back."

The image of Leigh Anne's mom froze and moved to a corner of the screen. The newscaster came back on. "Ms. Antonia was able to get away from the device without being seriously injured, but who knows if others will be so lucky. A spokesperson from Dream Dry gave us the following statement: 'We apologize for the unfortunate experience Ms. Antonia had with our product. Rest assured we are investigating the situation and will do whatever we can to make sure our product is safe.'"

The newscaster straightened the papers on her desk and shifted in her chair to look at another camera. The image of Leigh Anne's mom was replaced by that of a two-story house. "Sales of new homes rose slightly last month," she said.

Tracy clicked off the television and ran to the bathroom. When she returned, she looked at Lindy expectantly. "Well, are we rich?"

"What?" said Lindy. "I don't know. The market's closed."

"The market's *closed*?" Tracy asked.

"Yeah, it closed at four."

"*Four?* When does it reopen?"

"Tomorrow morning."

Tracy's face took on a look between sadness and disbelief that was so tragic, it made Lindy crack up. "Don't worry," she said. "Hopefully, the news will get around tonight. And by tomorrow, the stock will be ready to plunge."

Chapter 29

Announcement Effect

The news did get around. It was on the second page of the *Star-Ledger* in the morning, with a big picture of Leigh Anne's mom staring grimly out at the viewer, a 130-Z in her hands. When Lindy googled Dream Dry after her shower, she found a one-paragraph article in the *Wall Street Journal* saying Dream Dry might need to recall the 130-Z, which, according to the article, was backed by a "leading venture capital group." And by the time she went to the computer lab during lunch, the article was now on the *Wall Street Journal* home page with the headline "Product Recall Threatens Dream Product." She read the article hungrily, devouring details about how Leigh Anne's mother wasn't the only one whose blow-dryer began to spark. Apparently, at least five other people who had been given the blow-dryer early had problems, and now a hairdresser in New Mexico was in the hospital with severe burns. Dream Dry was officially recalling the 130-Z and "postponing the much-anticipated launch until further notice."

Lindy e-mailed the article to Tracy along with the latest stock quote; DDRY was down to $32.32. It had dropped 31 percent in half a day, and the news was only just getting big. She knew she should feel sorry for that hairdresser in New Mexico, but she mostly felt giddy with anticipation. She had already made back more than half the money she'd lost. *Please,* she prayed, *let DDRY drop just another ten dollars. Then I'll have made back every last penny.*

Lindy and Tracy couldn't concentrate on homework that afternoon. They watched CNBC until their mom got home from work. A crazy man threw things at the screen and called for people to "Sell! Sell Sell!" And a curly haired newscaster expressed her own disappointment at the failure of the Dream Dry 130-Z. "I guess I'll still have to hold out for the next revolution in hair care," she said with a sigh.

Their mother walked in to find them hugging and jumping up and down. It was incredibly suspicious, but Tracy thought on the fly and said she was teaching Lindy a new dance that she couldn't *believe* Lindy didn't know yet. "Lindy should thank me for bringing her into the twenty-first century," she said. "If anyone at her school found out she hadn't even heard of the Jump Hug, it'd be social suicide."

By the time the market closed, DDRY was down to $23.90. Both girls were anxious to get out, but Lindy convinced Tracy to hold tight; she was sure the stock wouldn't pull any dramatic comebacks. She programmed the trading site to automatically end her position if DDRY went back up to twenty-five dollars, just in case. Since it was likely to drop more tomorrow while she was in school, she also put in an order for the program to end the short when DDRY reached twenty-one dollars. She had a feeling it could go even lower—which would mean she'd make even more money—but she wouldn't let herself get greedy. That was what got her into trouble in the first place. She'd lucked out so far with how big this Dream Dry news got; the responsible thing to do was be thankful, take her winnings, and walk away—forever.

Lindy couldn't focus in her morning classes. She crossed her fingers when the clock struck nine thirty a.m. At lunchtime, she walked to the computer lab and looked up the price of DDRY. A grin slowly grew on her face as she saw the stock quote: $19.50. She sank into the chair and breathed an enormous sigh of relief. She could just picture Tracy, halfway across town in the computer lab at the high school, doing the same exact thing. With one well-placed bet, one lucky move, they had made back every cent of the money Lindy had lost.

Lindy was so happy, so relieved, and so overwhelmed by the potential consequences—now averted—of what she'd done in the first place, she logged off the computer, walked to the girls' bathroom, locked herself in a stall, and cried.

ELISSA BRENT WEISSMAN

PART THREE

Chapter 30
Delivery

Lindy told Cassie about her close call, but not until a few weeks later, after she had sold all her stocks and stuck to her promise of not looking back.

Steph and Howe were still in their own mushy bubble of happiness, but Lindy didn't care. She and Cassie ate lunch together every day and hung out after school a few times a week. The bond she'd formed with Tracy during those tense few days hadn't wavered; they were getting along so well, their parents were almost suspicious. And even though she'd gotten out of all her positions and not logged in to the trading account once since that fateful day, the few times Lindy did check out the news headlines, it seemed like the market was very volatile, and she was glad to not have to think about it.

After she heard the story, Cassie asked, "Do you think you'll ever trade stocks again?"

They were at Lindy's house, eating popcorn and watching video clips online instead of doing their math homework.

"I don't know," Lindy said. She licked some butter off her fingers. "It is really exciting, and for a while I was really good at it. Maybe when I'm an adult and really rich."

"But you wouldn't risk all your money."

"No way. Just a little bit of it. I'd want to stay rich."

"No offense," said Cassie. "But you really lucked out."

"Oh, I know," Lindy said. She opened her eyes wide and shook her head. "Believe me. I'm just glad it's all over."

The doorbell rang, and Tracy shouted from behind the closed door of her bedroom. "I'll get it!"

But Lindy had already pushed herself up from laying on the floor. "That's okay," she said. "I'll go get it."

"No!" Tracy's door flew open, but she didn't come out of her room. Lindy could hear her running around. "Let me get it."

Lindy looked at Cassie with raised eyebrows. Now she needed to know who Tracy was expecting. "Don't worry," she shouted casually. "Cassie and I will get the door." Cassie's mouth dropped open, and Lindy laughed. She ran into the hall and waved for Cassie to follow.

ELISSA BRENT WEISSMAN

"Don't you dare, Lind!" said Tracy.

The two sisters sprinted down the hall. Tracy tried to push past Lindy, who put her arms out to try to fend her off. In the living room, Tracy grabbed the back of Lindy's shirt and pulled her on to the couch. The doorbell rang again.

"Who is it?" Lindy shouted.

Tracy shot her a stern look, straightened her shirt, fluffed her hair, and reached for the handle.

A woman's voice carried through the door. "Process server."

Three heads cocked to the side: Cassie's from the entrance to the living room, Lindy's from the couch, and Tracy's at the door.

"Who?" Tracy asked.

"Process server," the woman repeated. "For Gary Sachs."

"What's that?" Lindy whispered. "Someone for Dad?"

"I have no idea," Tracy whispered back. She walked to the living room window and peeked out through the curtains. "It's a woman in a suit," she said. "Maybe she works with Dad."

"Don't open it," said Lindy.

The doorbell rang once more.

Tracy walked back to the door and paused with her hand over the knob. Then she turned it and opened the door. A petite woman in a navy blue suit and high beige heels stood there. "Hello," she said. "Is Mr. Sachs in?"

"No," said Tracy. "I mean, he's not available at the moment."

Lindy rose from the couch and hovered behind Tracy so that she could see the woman.

"I'm a process server, here to serve him some legal papers. May I leave them with you?" She held out a legal-size envelope.

"Um," Tracy said, "I guess." She took the envelope and looked at the name and address on it. It was for their dad, all right.

"And may I have your name, please?" the woman said.

"Tracy," said Tracy.

"Thank you, Tracy. Please see to it that Mr. Sachs receives the papers." She smiled at Lindy, then turned and walked briskly to a sleek, black car parked on the street.

The three girls looked at one another. "What was that?" Lindy asked.

"I have no idea," said Tracy.

"Is Dad in trouble?" Lindy asked.

"It's probably just something for work," Tracy said. But Lindy could tell she was nervous too. Their dad had never had something work-related delivered to the house before, and he'd never had a visit from someone so serious-looking before.

"I should probably go home," said Cassie.

"You don't have to," said Lindy. There was no reason for Cassie to leave, really; the contents of the envelope could be perfectly harmless. And besides, their dad wouldn't be home to open it for a few hours. But its delivery had changed the mood, and Lindy knew that if Cassie stayed, they wouldn't have much fun. The arrival of the envelope, which Tracy now left on the coffee table before disappearing back into her room, had sucked the fun out of the afternoon.

"It's okay," said Cassie. "Call me later, if you can. Or I'll just talk to you tomorrow."

As Lindy watched Cassie leave through the glass door, another car pulled into the driveway. This one was not sleek and black, but big, old, and dented. Wheezing and rumbling, it puttered to a stop, and then the noise died suddenly. Lindy hoped it hadn't turned off for good. When the driver got out, Lindy smirked. It was a tall, gangly boy with messy dark hair that he had to push away from his eyes. He was holding a folder, but it wasn't nearly as official-looking as the envelope they'd just received. This had to be who Tracy was expecting. And he was driving, so he had to be at least sixteen.

"Hey," he said when he reached the doorstep. "This is for Tracy." He held up the folder.

A bad sister would take the folder and let the boy leave. A great sister would go get Tracy without asking any questions. Lindy was content to be a good sister: She told the boy to hold on, but not before getting his name.

On her way to Tracy's room, her eyes were pulled to the envelope from the process server. Her stomach churned as she wondered what was inside.

ELISSA BRENT WEISSMAN

Chapter 31
Insider Trading

"You told me you haven't been trading."

"I haven't! I haven't made a single trade lately."

"Nothing in the online account?"

"Nothing, honey. I haven't even *looked* at that account since before the new year."

Lindy and Tracy leaned against opposite walls in the hallway, listening to their parents argue in the kitchen. Lindy looked at her sister with wide, frightened eyes. They didn't know the contents of the envelope, but it clearly related to stock trading, and it sounded bad. Really bad.

"These investigations usually take years," Mr. Sachs said. "This could be about something I traded ten years ago. Not that I had any money to trade ten years ago . . ."

"It's not from ten years ago, Gary," said Mrs. Sachs. "It's

from the beginning of January. It has the date right here."

"I never heard of something like this coming to light so quickly. Maybe that date's a mistake."

"I'm hoping this whole thing's a mistake!"

Mr. Sachs put his arms around his wife, but she remained stiff. "It's got to be a mistake," he said. "I told you I haven't been doing any trading at all, let alone any illegal short selling!"

Tracy stared at Lindy. "Illegal short selling?" she mouthed.

Lindy shook her head and shrugged nervously. Had her short sale been illegal?

"I barely know how to buy and sell simple stocks. I wouldn't even know how to do this sort of evil-genius insider trading stuff."

Lindy swallowed. *Evil genius?* She peeked into the kitchen.

"I can assure you"—Mr. Sachs took the letter from his wife's stiff fingers and read from the first page—"that I have not violated Section 17(a) of the Securities Act of 1933, or Section 10(b) of the Securities Exchange Act of 1934." He smiled at her. "Don't you think those acts are a little out-dated, anyway?"

Mrs. Sachs didn't smile back.

"They must be looking for a different Gary Sachs. Think

about how many Gary Sachses are in this world. Maybe they meant to send it to *Goldman* Sachs, the big investment bank."

Or maybe just a different Sachs, Lindy thought, her stomach sinking.

Mrs. Sachs refused to be amused. "Call them up and get it straightened out."

"I will. It's too late now, but I will call this number first thing in the morning."

"Maybe you should call a lawyer first," Mrs. Sachs said.

Tracy winced, and Lindy felt tears coming. Their dad needed a lawyer? Was he going to go to jail?

"Maybe," Mr. Sachs said. "I guess it can't hurt to have a lawyer call them, just in case."

"Call your sister," Mrs. Sachs said.

"She deals with child custody cases, honey. I don't think she knows a thing about insider trading."

"She might know someone."

"Okay," said Mr. Sachs. "But first, I'm going to log in to my account and see what's been going on. See if there's a record of these trades on the dates they give here. Maybe someone hacked the account."

Tracy and Lindy stared at each other.

"What do we do?" Tracy whispered.

"I don't know," Lindy whispered back.

Their dad passed between them to go down the hall and get the laptop. "Hi, girls," he said.

"What's going on, Dad?" Tracy asked.

"Nothing to worry about, sweetie. Just a misunderstanding involving some stocks."

"What sort of misunderstanding?" Lindy asked.

Their mother came into the hall. "Don't worry about it, girls. Just let Daddy sort it out."

Lindy's tears started flowing. Their mom never referred to their dad as "daddy" unless something was wrong. "Are you going to go to jail?" Lindy asked.

Her dad laughed, but her mother didn't. She looked like she wanted to know the answer too.

"Of course I'm not going to jail!" Mr. Sachs said. He gave Lindy a kiss on the top of her head. "Come on," he said, mostly to his wife. "The Securities and Exchange Commission thinks I made some trades that weren't legal. But I haven't made any trades in months, which I'm going to show your mother right now."

Tracy elbowed Lindy sharply in the side as they followed their parents to the dining room table, where their dad brought up the trading website and logged in. Lindy knew she should say something, but she just couldn't bring herself to yet. She watched and waited, her heart pounding against her ribs.

"See this number here?" Mr. Sachs said, pointing to the amount of money in the account. "The account value is just about what I remember it being the last time I logged in. So I didn't make millions of dollars with this illegal trading, at any rate. What a shame," he joked.

No one laughed. Lindy could barely breathe.

Her dad whistled as he opened the account and clicked to view past transactions. The tune changed to a low single note when he saw the activity from a month ago.

"What's that?" Mrs. Sachs asked.

"Well," he replied. He moved closer to the screen, then sighed and leaned back. "The account did make thirty thousand dollars a few weeks ago by shorting this stock—DDRY. It looks like . . ." He scrolled through the list of transactions. "It looks like we lost about that much, and then someone made it all back in a couple days with this short."

"Someone?" said Mrs. Sachs. "Someone who? *Someone* was just *playing* with *our* money?"

"Someone must have hacked into our account," Mr. Sachs said. "Though it's strange that they'd make all this money and then just leave it here. I think we do need a lawyer after all."

Mrs. Sachs gave a high-pitched cry and rubbed her face.

Tracy pulled her hand from Lindy, who had been gripping it so hard, she was beginning to cut off the circulation.

"This is so bizarre," Mr. Sachs said, frowning at the screen and rubbing his beard. "I don't know how this happened."

"But you didn't do it?"

"I didn't do it," Mr. Sachs said, his voice full of wonder. "It happened in my account, but they have the wrong person."

Lindy mustered up all her courage. "That's true," she said. "They're looking for me."

Chapter 32
Long and Short

Three days later, the family sat around the dining room table with Francine Hawthorne, an attorney who specialized in securities law. She was a stern-looking woman with dark brown hair swept tightly from her face. Her brown eyes were serious and piercing behind her frameless glasses, and her mouth stayed in a straight line, never revealing even the hint of a smile or a frown.

Lindy had already told her parents the whole story, and she'd also told it to Ms. Hawthorne. Now Ms. Hawthorne was here to tell them just how bad the situation was.

"I'm not going to lie to you," Ms. Hawthorne said. "This case is a sticky one."

"Lindy's just twelve—" Mrs. Sachs said.

"But she was trading with an account in the name of

Gary Sachs," Ms. Hawthorne interrupted. "And he is not twelve. But let's backtrack. Here's the long and short of it." Ms. Hawthorne chuckled. "Securities law joke," she said. When no one laughed, she continued. "The Securities and Exchange Commission, or the SEC, was established shortly after the Great Depression to regulate the stock market. It's still in place today, and it makes sure no one is profiting by doing illegal things that end up hurting investors or the economy. This letter means that Mr. Sachs is being investigated by the SEC's Division of Enforcement, for two things: insider trading and illegal short selling.

"The SEC has really been cracking down on both of these things. You may have seen some cases in the newspaper recently involving insider trading. Maybe you've heard of Christopher Knight?"

Lindy and Tracy stared at her blankly, but their parents both nodded.

"He was the assistant at that train company," Mr. Sachs said.

"Yes," said Ms. Hawthorne. "He was an assistant to the CEO of Central Pacific Rail Lines, and he knew that the company was going to merge with Northern Rail, which would make the price of their stock go way up. So he bought a large amount of stock at a low price. When the merger was announced, the stock did soar, and he sold all his shares to make a profit of almost one million dollars. He made all that money based on information that he only knew because he worked there, and that information was supposed to be kept private. That is why the SEC prosecuted him for insider trading."

Lindy was bursting with questions. Now that she knew what insider trading was and that it was against the law, she understood why Christopher Knight had gotten in trouble. But she didn't work for Dream Dry, and she didn't know the information she had was supposed to be private. It seemed like the difference was clear, but she was too intimidated by Ms. Hawthorne to say anything.

Luckily, her mother wasn't. "Lindy doesn't work for Dream Dry; she's in seventh grade, for Pete's sake. And she didn't have access to any confidential information. She only heard what had happened to someone who lives in this town—that's public gossip, not top-secret company information."

Ms. Hawthorne pulled her lips straighter into what Lindy thought might be an attempt at a smile. "No, Lindy does not work for Dream Dry. Christopher Knight committed insider trading in the most traditional sense. He was what the law considers a 'corporate insider,' because he worked at the company and had direct access to confidential information. But there are two important situations that also classify as insider trading. One is that someone can become a 'temporary insider' by conducting business with the corporation. So if a company hires another company to do their advertising, those advertising executives become temporary insiders. Or if the company hires an accountant or a lawyer from an outside firm, that account or lawyer can become a temporary insider. So when a company's stock price sharply rises or falls, the SEC will look to see who made trades prior to the big announcement, and then give a list of those names to the company to see if they recognize anyone."

"So?" said Mrs. Sachs. "Lindy was not hired in any capacity at Dream Dry. Why would they recognize her name?"

"They wouldn't. But remember that as far as the paperwork is concerned, Lindy Sachs wasn't doing the trading, Gary Sachs was. And they would recognize Gary Sachs's name, because he worked for Dream Dry."

Everyone looked at Mr. Sachs. He cocked his head and squinted. "I'm sorry?" he said.

"According to the SEC," Ms. Hawthorne said, "your company, Excellence Consulting, has been working with Dream Dry since last August."

"We have?" he said.

"You didn't know that?" Ms. Hawthorne asked.

Mr. Sachs shook his head, raised his eyebrows. "We have five hundred employees in our office. We have people working with more than fifty businesses at any given time. If you're not put on a project, you could have no way of knowing it's going on."

Ms. Hawthorne was taking copious notes on what Mr. Sachs was saying. "And you were never put on the Dream Dry project? The company recognized your name from the list, so it must have been in their records somehow."

"Dream Dry . . ." Mr. Sachs scratched his chin through his beard. "Oh wait. They make all sorts of shampoos and things, right? Blow-dryers, other hair thingamajigs?"

"Dad," said Tracy. "How can you not have heard of Dream Dry?"

"They don't make shampoo?"

"They do! And tons of other stuff," Tracy said. "Don't you use Dream Dry shampoo, Mom?"

"Yes," said Mrs. Sachs. "You use it too, Gary. You look at the bottle every day when you apply it to your hair."

Mr. Sachs snapped his fingers. "I knew that logo looked familiar!"

Lindy's eyes widened. She asked Ms. Hawthorne, "Can you be a temporary insider if you use Dream Dry shampoo?"

"No, no," her dad said quickly. "I did work on the Dream Dry project; just for a few days. It was months ago. They hired Excellence Consulting to help them with their employee benefits. I knew that logo looked familiar when I got there, but I couldn't place it!"

"You couldn't place the logo that was on the bottle you used for shampoo that morning," said Tracy, shaking her head. "Dad."

But Ms. Hawthorne stayed focused. "So you were on the project?"

"I went to their office just once or twice," Mr. Sachs said, "and then a bigger project came up at another company, and they needed more experienced people to work on that. So I got moved to that, and Heather Perkins took over for me at Dream Dry. She was very excited," he remembered. "Maybe she knew that she uses their shampoo!"

"Most people would," Tracy muttered.

Ms. Hawthorne was on to her second page of notes. "So we can get proof from Excellence Consulting that you only worked at Dream Dry for a few days, right when the project started?"

"Of course," said Mr. Sachs.

"Do you speak to Heather Perkins regularly or to anyone else who is still working there?"

"No," said Mr. Sachs. "I never see Heather. I didn't even realize that project was still going on."

 Ms. Hawthorne wrote that down.

"So everything should be okay, then?" Lindy asked. "Since my dad wasn't there?"

"Well," said Ms. Hawthorne, "like I said, there are *two* other important situations that can be considered insider trading. Even if we clear the temporary insider charge from Mr. Sachs's company, there is also a possibility," she continued, "that Ms."—she checked her notes—"Antonia, who had the incident with the blow-dryer, could be considered to have had access to confidential Dream Dry information, and acting on that information was therefore against the law."

"That's ridiculous," Lindy's mother said. "Dream Dry didn't let her in on a company secret—they electrocuted her with their blow-dryer!"

"Go, Mom," Tracy said, and Lindy smiled. She knew kids whose moms argued like this with teachers over a bad grade; her mom would *never* do that. But she was proud and grateful to see how fiercely her mom was prepared to defend her when it came to being prosecuted by the Securities and Exchange Commission. She also sank low in her chair, feeling guilty. Her mom was willing to defend her like this, even when she'd gotten them into all this trouble.

Ms. Hawthorne gave her signature tight-lipped smile. "It can be seen as ridiculous," she granted. "And that is what we will try to prove. But the SEC will try to prove that it's not, that the trade that took place was against the law. And even if we can dodge the insider trading bullet, the SEC has another piece of ammunition that we haven't discussed yet. Illegal short selling."

"Is all short selling illegal?" Mr. Sachs asked.

"Not necessarily," said Ms. Hawthorne. "The SEC began regulating short selling after the market crashed in 2008 because big investment companies discovered that they could use short selling to start a cycle that would make them lots of money. For example, let's say there's a big investment company called"—she looked at her paperwork and saw the name of the Sachses' street—"Millford Court. And Millford Court has thousands of employees and invests millions of dollars in stocks every day. One day Millford Court decides to take a short position on, say, McDonald's."

"Like, McDonald's McDonald's?" said Tracy. "Happy Meals?"

"Exactly," said Ms. Hawthorne. "For the sake of our example, Millford Court decides that they think McDonald's stock is going to go down in value, so they short it. But since they're Millford Court, they don't just short McDonald's stock for a little bit of money; they short it for five million dollars. They basically bet five million dollars that McDonald's is going to do badly."

"Whoa," said Lindy.

"That's what other big investors say," said Ms. Hawthorne. "They see that Millford Court thinks McDonald's is going to do badly, and they start to think, *Millford Court usually knows what they're doing. If they think McDonald's is going to do badly, they must know something we don't.* So these other big investment companies decide to sell their shares and get out now. They sell off millions of dollars of their shares."

"And because they do that," Lindy said, catching on, "the stock starts to go down."

"Exactly," said Ms. Hawthorne. "When people start selling, the value gets lower. And once the value starts dropping, other people see it and say, 'Uh-oh, McDonald's stock is dropping quickly. I'd better sell now.' And that starts a cycle."

"But Millford Court makes a lot of money," said Lindy, nodding at the way the system and the hypothetical plan worked. "Because they were betting that it'd go down."

"But they made it go down," Tracy said, "by betting that."

"Right," said Ms. Hawthorne. "And it isn't fair to do that to McDonald's or to any other company. Investment firms were doing this, and it started to get out of hand. So the SEC began to regulate it, to make short selling illegal."

"But I didn't know about any of that," Lindy said. "I just knew I'd read something about making money when a stock went down, so when Tracy told me about what happened to Leigh Anne's mom—I mean, Ms. Antonia—I guessed that the stock would go down, and I shorted it."

"Right," said Mrs. Sachs. "It's all just a big misunderstanding. I am not condoning Lindy's behavior—what she did was thoughtless and dangerous and stupid."

Lindy sniffed and looked at her lap.

"But," her mother continued, "she isn't a big investment bank looking to make millions by maliciously destroying another company. She was a just a girl who made, what seems to me, a smart business decision. She didn't know it wasn't legal."

"And thirty thousand dollars is a lot of money for us," Mr. Sachs added. "But it's hardly millions. Is it usual for the SEC to come after someone who made such a relatively small amount of money? And to do it so quickly? That Christopher Knight case you mentioned happened at least five years ago, and it's only coming out now."

Ms. Hawthorne said, "In light of the Christopher Knight case and some others, the SEC is really trying to crack down on insider trading, to respond swiftly and harshly. Thirty-thousand dollars is enough to raise red flags. It's not millions, but oftentimes they'll pursue a relatively small case like yours in order to set an example, to show that this is illegal for everyone and no one can expect to get away with it."

"My English teacher does that," Tracy said, rolling her eyes. "You can't get away with copying even *one sentence* of someone else's homework in that class." Her mother gave her a sharp look, and she quickly added, "Not that I know from personal experience."

"Good," said Mrs. Sachs.

"Geez," Tracy muttered. "And apparently, in this family, you can get in trouble for just *mentioning* copying home-work when someone else is being investigated by the *government*."

"Shut up, Trace," Lindy said.

"Lindy," warned her father.

"She doesn't have to rub it in," Lindy said.

"I'm just stating the obvious," Tracy said.

"So why state it?" Lindy said.

"Girls!" their mother said.

Ms. Hawthorne, who was watching all this without giving away a trace of emotion, cleared her throat. "We have our work cut out for us," she said. "I'll speak with the SEC first and explain the situation. There's a chance that when I tell them it was a seventh grader who did the trading, they'll drop the investigation without a hearing."

"Do you think so?" Lindy asked hopefully.

"Honestly," said Ms. Hawthorne, "no. We have a potential insider trading connection with Mr. Sachs's company, and with whatever arrangement Ms. Antonia had when she agreed to test the blow-dryer. The illegal short sale adds another layer of complication. And most importantly, we'll have to prove that it was, in fact, Lindy who made the trade on her own, and not Gary Sachs making up a story to get away with his actions for free."

"Free?" said Mr. Sachs.

"Right now, the investigation is to see if they want to bring a civil case against you," Ms. Hawthorne said. "That means that if we lose, all you'll owe is the profit Lindy made, plus a fine for three times that amount—so, a total of about one hundred and twenty thousand dollars."

Mrs. Sachs looked like Ms. Hawthorne had thrown a bucket of ice water on her. "Oh, that's all," she said.

"But there's also the small possibility that the U.S. Department of Justice could decide to pursue this with a criminal case, in which case Mr. Sachs could be facing up to ten years in jail."

"But he didn't do anything!" Lindy cried. "It was me. And I didn't know any of it was illegal." She grabbed her dad's hand, and he gave it a gentle squeeze.

Ms. Hawthorne's voice and expression softened for the first time since she arrived. "I know," she said gently. "And together we're going to convince the SEC."

Chapter 33
Entropy

"I bet they'll drop the case," Tracy said for the fifth time in about as many minutes.

Her mother pressed the iron down onto the collar of a shirt, making steam rise in big puffs. "Tracy," she said.

"I mean, come on," Tracy said. "The SEC isn't going to investigate a seventh grader. It'll look ridiculous."

"I don't know what they'll do," Mrs. Sachs said. "There's no way we can predict it."

"They have to drop it," Tracy said, "don't you think, Lind?"

Lindy, who was lying on the couch, shrugged and continued staring at the ceiling. She didn't know what to think. Ms. Hawthorne had called the house yesterday to say she'd spoken with someone from the SEC and told them Lindy's

ELISSA BRENT WEISSMAN

story. They were going to deliberate and be in touch sometime today with their decision as to whether or not to continue with the investigation.

Mr. Sachs had gone into work that morning as usual, but Lindy and Tracy had stayed home from school to wait for the news. It was hard to argue that they had to go to school when their mother took the day off too, claiming she wouldn't be able to concentrate until she knew what was going on. It seemed the only thing she was able to concentrate on was ironing; she'd been ironing for almost two hours now. When she'd finished the pile of shirts that needed to be done, she'd moved on to shirts that were already hanging in the closet.

"Though, if they dropped it, we'd probably have heard by now," Tracy said. "I think it'd take less time to let us know about that, but it's taking a long time."

"Yes, it is," Mrs. Sachs said. She looked at the clock. "You girls could have gone to school."

"Oh well," said Tracy.

"I'll go to school tomorrow," said Lindy, "even if we haven't heard anything yet." She meant it too. Sitting in class and wondering whether or not the case would be dropped would be better than sitting at home listening to Tracy talk about whether or not the case would be dropped.

"Ugh, can you imagine?" Tracy said. She plopped down on the couch by Lindy's feet. "We *have* to hear today, or I'm going to go insane."

"I think you've already gone insane."

"You might be right," Tracy admitted. "Right now, I'm wishing Jackie would arrive with my homework already. It'll give me something to do."

The doorbell rang, and all three of them startled.

"Wow," said Lindy said, raising her eyebrows. "I hope you're wishing the case was dropped too."

Tracy crossed her fingers and looked around as if waiting for a sign. When nothing happened, she joined her mother at the front door.

"Who is it?" Mrs. Sachs asked.

"Process server," came the voice from the other side.

Lindy bolted upright. Her mother took a breath and opened the door.

A man in a long black coat and leather gloves stood at the door. He was holding an envelope that looked frighteningly familiar. "Hello," he said. "Is Ms. Melinda Sachs in?"

Lindy rose slowly from the couch and walked, zombie-like, to stand between her mother and sister at the door. "That's me," she said.

The man tried hard to keep his face neutral as he handed

her the envelope. "Melinda Sachs, you are hereby subpoenaed to appear before the Securities and Exchange Commission."

Lindy gulped as she took the envelope from him. Ms. Hawthorne had warned that this could happen, but she hadn't realized until just this moment how much she'd been thinking, like Tracy, that it wouldn't.

This envelope meant that the SEC had not decided to drop the investigation. They had decided to investigate Lindy.

Her mother put her arm across her shoulders, and Lindy sniffed. She stood there feeling numb and hollow; she knew her body was still standing in the doorway, but she was somehow detached from it. *I'm being investigated by the government,* she thought very calmly. *What is going to happen now?*

It wasn't until the process server had turned around and begun to walk down the walkway that any of three Sachs women saw what was in the street. Five news vans, a slew of cars, and a crowd of photographers, reporters, and cameramen.

"Whoa," said Tracy.

"Um, Mom?" said Lindy.

"Ms. Sachs!" shouted a reporter, rushing up the walkway. "Which one of you is Melinda? How does it feel to be the youngest person to ever be investigated by the SEC?"

Lindy stared at the advancing crowd with her face frozen in shock.

"Ms. Sachs!" called another reporter. "How long have you been trading stocks online?"

"Ms. Sachs!" shouted another. "How did you know to short Dream Dry?"

"Ms. Sachs!"

"Ms. Sachs!"

"Melinda!"

Lindy kept staring at the mob as her mother and Tracy pulled her inside, closed the door, and locked it behind them.

Chapter 34
Defensive Strategy

According to the SEC's website—Lindy read it three times—all investigations were conducted privately. So much for that.

No one knew how the word got out about the investigation, but that didn't matter—the word was out. The family stopped answering the phone after the fourth reporter called, but it kept ringing endlessly until Lindy's mom disconnected the lines. News vans blocked Mr. Sachs from pulling into the driveway when he got home from work, so he had to park down the street and force his way through the crowd and questions to get in his own front door. "At least I won't have to face this coming home tomorrow," he said at dinner.

"Why not?" Mrs. Sachs asked.

"Because my boss asked me to stay home until after

everything is settled," Mr. Sachs said. "He knows I didn't do anything, but it looks better for the company if I just lay low until after it all blows over."

Mrs. Sachs didn't say anything, and Lindy didn't cry, but most of their dinner went uneaten.

Even though none of them had said anything to any of the reporters, the story was still on all the major news stations that night, complete with images of Lindy standing outside the door with the envelope in her hands.

The news story made it so that the crowd outside the Sachses' house was even bigger the next morning. Their mom drove Lindy and Tracy to school—trying to walk would have been like trying to walk through a flock of homing pigeons—where there were, thankfully, no news crews waiting to follow them to their lockers.

Lindy was glad no one in her class ever listened to her social studies teacher's pleas that they be more in touch with current events. None of the kids in her classes asked her about the case, and only a couple people looked twice at her in the cafeteria or the hallway. She could tell that her teachers seemed to know from the way they looked at her, but only her English teacher pulled her aside and asked how she was doing. She was able to confide the details to Cassie during lunch while everyone else at the table was absorbed in helping Jessica decide what breed of dog to get.

It was a good thing she'd told Cassie too. By the end of the day, the news crews were waiting just off school grounds after eighth period. The principal made sure they didn't step foot on school property, but she couldn't ensure that they wouldn't follow Lindy as she walked home. Luckily, Cassie's mother worked nearby and was able to come pick them both up. The two girls sprinted from the school to the car carrying big pieces of poster board from the art room to block their faces.

All the commotion meant Lindy could forget about the kids at school being normal around her again tomorrow.

Ms. Hawthorne came over that night and taught Lindy and her family the two most important words until this whole ordeal was over: "no comment."

"You say it whenever someone from the press asks you *anything*," she said firmly. "You say it when coworkers mention the case. You say it when friends ask you about the case. Heck, you say it when anyone outside the five people in this room bring up the case. *No comment*."

"Does it have to be 'no comment,'" Tracy said, "or can it be something else that means the same thing?"

"It could be something similar," said Ms. Hawthorne. "'I have no comment at this time,' for instance, or 'I'm not at liberty to discuss that.' But 'no comment' is easy because it's only two words."

"Well, I was thinking of short ones too," Tracy said. "Like, 'Go away.'"

"Well," said Ms. Hawthorne, "it's best to be courteous."

"Bummer," said Tracy. "I was also thinking of using 'Shove it.'"

Lindy laughed. "Buzz off," she suggested.

"Get lost!" Tracy said with a laugh.

"Scram!" Lindy said in her best Oscar the Grouch voice.

"Girls," their mom said with a sigh. She pressed her pale palms into her eyes.

"Yes, girls," their dad said. "Let's be serious about this."

Lindy and Tracy tried to stifle their laughs.

"We could say, 'Out of my face!'" their dad yelled.

Lindy and Tracy cracked up. Ms. Hawthorne's face stayed stern, but her shoulders started shaking, which only made Lindy laugh harder.

"Beat it," their dad sang, "just beat it!" He stood up and started snapping and dancing around the living room.

Lindy laughed so hard, she slid out of her chair, which made Tracy double over and crumple, hysterical, into a ball on the floor. Trying to catch her breath, Lindy saw that even her mother had cracked a smile, and she felt, just for a moment, that maybe everything would be all right.

ELISSA BRENT WEISSMAN

Chapter 35
Inside Days

The SEC hearing wasn't for two weeks, and Lindy felt torn in half. Part of her wanted to get the hearing over with as quickly as possible, and that part of her felt like time had slowed down to a crawl. The other part of her wanted to pretend that everything was normal, and that part of her felt like the days were rushing by at lightning speed, barreling toward the hearing. Ms. Hawthorne said she'd go over some practice questions with her the night before, so she'd know what to expect. Apart from that, Ms. Hawthorne said there were only two things she could do to prepare: (1) Ignore the reporters, and (2) Not be nervous.

Lindy hoped number one would get easier with time—if she never answered their questions, the reporters should eventually get bored and go away. Number two was so impossible that Lindy didn't even bother trying.

It took only one day of ignoring the reporters to make most of them leave Lindy and her family alone. But it didn't make them leave the story alone. Headlines plastered the covers and home pages of all the newspapers Lindy read when she was trading: the *Wall Street Journal*, the *New York Times*, the *Washington Post*, and even the *Financial Times* in London.

SEC INVESTIGATES TWELVE-YEAR-OLD GIRL FOR

INSIDER TRADING

•

SEVENTH-GRADE STOCK GENIUS SUBPOENAED BY SEC

•

FOUR-FOOT-SIX DAY TRADER GIVES NEW MEANING

TO SHORT SELLING

At least these articles got most of the limited details they had correct. You couldn't tune in to CNN, CNBC, or local news stations without hearing about the story as well, and they weren't always accurate. One got Lindy's hometown wrong; one claimed Lindy had made the trade from the computer lab at her high school; and two "experts" debated who actually made the trade: Mr. Sachs or his son.

The blogosphere was even worse. Even though their mother insisted they not read any of it, Tracy followed the feedback online like it was part of her homework. She'd call Lindy to her room to show her particularly outrageous blog entries. Lindy's favorite was one that expressed amazement that a fourth grader could make one million dollars from trading. Tracy's favorite was a reader comment on a New Jersey *Star-Ledger* article that said, "i no this girls sister and shes HOT."

With all the mistakes, Lindy could see the allure of all the offers she was getting to tell her side of the story. Book deals, radio interviews, appearances on late-night talk shows—Mrs. Sachs erased every message and threw away every piece of mail, but Ms. Hawthorne said to get used to it because there'd only be more offers after the hearing, once they knew the SEC's decision.

The hearing. The decision. Getting through reporters was going to be nothing compared to getting through the hearing. Lindy would have to convince the government that she made the trade, not her dad, and that she didn't do anything illegal.

Lindy had never liked public speaking. She dreaded class presentations, and she begged the chorus teacher not to make her do a solo. But this was so much worse than speaking in front of the class or singing in front of the auditorium. The stakes were higher than a bad grade or a wrong note. This was for real. And she was scared to death.

Chapter 36
Open Outcry

The hearing was on Tuesday at ten o'clock in the morning. Her dad had suggested they drive down to Washington, DC, on Saturday and make a vacation out of it—visit the monuments, go to the Smithsonian—but they decided against it, knowing they wouldn't be able to appreciate any of the sites. Instead, they were going to leave Monday afternoon. They wanted to spend as little time in Washington as possible.

Lindy's parents gave her and Tracy the option of staying home from school on Monday, but both of them decided to go. With the hearing just over twenty-four hours away, Lindy welcomed the opportunity to think about anything else. But all the whispers and stares as she walked down the hall in the morning made her wonder if she'd made the right choice.

She arrived at her locker and found a piece of paper stuck on with gum: a drawing of a stick figure behind bars.

She pulled the paper off, but the gum stretched out in long strands and got on her fingers. She tried to remove it with her other hand, but all she did was create a pink, sticky mess. She could hear kids laughing as she made her way to the girls' bathroom, but she held herself together. She was using a paper towel to wipe the gum off her hand when she heard talking coming from the stalls.

"Is her dad really going to go to jail?"

"Probably. It's actually kind of sad. He probably did it because they needed the money."

"Yeah. I mean, you can tell from her clothes."

"Her clothes aren't *that* bad. But you should see her house."

"Really?"

"Yeah, her parents can't afford anything. Lindy doesn't even have a cell phone."

Lindy stood stock-still, her hands covered in gum and her eyes filling with tears. That second voice was one she knew well—or at least *thought* she'd known well. It was Steph's.

One toilet flushed, then another. Lindy rubbed her hands together under the faucet so quickly that water splashed all over her shirt. She still had a piece of gum stuck to one thumb, but she didn't care. She just had to get out of there. The middle stall opened as she headed for the door, and for one painful second, her eyes met Steph's. Lindy bolted before she could see Steph's reaction. She didn't want to know if Steph wasn't sorry.

Lindy willed herself not to cry as she walked down the hall. She wanted to hide behind her locker door, but she couldn't get her lock to open.

"Lindy."

Lindy closed her eyes and breathed. It was another voice she hadn't heard in weeks. Howe's.

"Are you okay?"

What a stupid question, Lindy thought. She whirled around and faced him. "No, I'm not okay."

"What's wrong?"

"Ask your girlfriend," Lindy spat.

Howe turned a deep shade of purple. Lindy saw Steph coming, and she kept her face steady.

When Steph arrived, she looped her arm through Howe's. "Hi," she said.

Howe looked at Lindy, then at Steph. "What happened?" he asked.

"I honestly don't know," Lindy said. "I thought we were friends. But then I hear you in the bathroom, saying all this stuff about me. Like my family is poor, and my dad is going to jail. Stuff you don't know anything about."

"How could I know about it?" Steph said, removing her arm from Howe's and placing her hands on her hips. "You don't tell me anything."

"*I* don't tell *you* anything?" Lindy stepped away from her locker and crossed her arms. "You guys didn't even tell me you were going out!"

"How could I?" Steph said. "You were gone for a month, and then I was all excited to have you back, but whenever I tried to talk to you, you'd just ask to borrow my phone."

A small crowd was starting to form in the hall, but Lindy didn't care. "You invited me to that concert with you, and then you changed your mind because I'm not cool enough to hang out with your new friends."

"Maybe you're not!" Steph shouted. "Your mom wouldn't let you go, anyway, and your dad's a criminal. You used to be fun, but now all you care about is your stupid stock trading. Do you even have any friends anymore? You spend your lunch periods in the computer lab, like a loser. And Howe likes me more than he ever liked you."

Lindy gasped. Even Steph seemed surprised by the cruelness of what she'd said. They both stayed quiet for a second, and the crowd around them waited.

Lindy wanted to shoot back something just as mean. Something about Steph's shallowness, or her weight. Something she knew would hurt. But what came out instead was what she cared about most. "Is that true?" Lindy asked Howe.

Howe put up his hands. "Keep me out of this," he said. "I'm not getting involved."

Lindy snorted. "It's a little late for that." She looked at the two of them, standing together opposite her. "Thanks a lot." She kicked her locker and started walking toward her homeroom.

"Lindy, wait," Howe said.

Lindy shook her head, the tears forming again in her eyes. She could ignore all the media, and she could even stand the hurtful things Steph had said in the bathroom, since she knew they were false. But what about the rest of it? What if the other things Steph said were true?

She stopped outside her homeroom and leaned against the wall. Her face was a mess, her shirt was wet, and there was still gum on her thumb. She didn't know if she should walk into the classroom or out of the school and right back home. How was she going to get through the hearing if she couldn't even have the courage to get through school? How could she face the Securities and Exchange Commission if she wasn't even strong enough to stand up to her supposed best friend?

A familiar body appeared next to her against the wall. It was Cassie, and she put her arm around Lindy's shoulder. "It's okay," Cassie said. "She doesn't know what she's talking about."

"Really?"

"Really."

Lindy looked at Cassie through her tears. She didn't know about the rest of it, but at least Steph was wrong about one thing. She did have a friend.

Chapter 37

Junior Corporation

Her family drove to Washington that afternoon and checked into a hotel. Lindy normally loved staying in hotels, but now she could barely appreciate anything about it. Having her own queen bed with the hotel sheets tucked supertight, the little bottles of bodywash and lotion in the bathroom; none of it could calm her nerves. She and Tracy went down to the hotel pool, but they just splashed around halfheartedly for ten minutes before going back up to the room.

Ms. Hawthorne met them for dinner that night to prep Lindy and her dad for what to expect, but Lindy couldn't concentrate. Her father was trying to be relaxed about it, but he kept rubbing his beard and saying "Yes, yes," even when there was nothing to say yes about. That made Lindy extra nervous.

Somehow she managed to fall asleep that night, and she woke up to find her dad sitting on the edge of her bed in his pajamas.

"Today's the day," he said softly with a small smile. "How are you feeling?"

Lindy wrinkled her forehead and looked at him apprehensively.

Mr. Sachs nodded. "Me too. Listen, Lind." He edged closer to her. "I don't know what will happen today, but whatever it is—whatever they decide—everything works out for the best in the end."

"I'm sorry, Dad," Lindy said, her voice full of sleep. "I didn't mean to get you into trouble."

"Oh really? Ever since you were a baby, I've had the sneaky feeling you were someday going to frame me for insider trading."

Lindy giggled.

Her dad gave her a kiss on the forehead. "I know, honey. Whatever happens, we're in this together."

Lindy took a big breath and sat up. She said, "Thanks, Dad."

"But before you get ready, you have to tell me one thing, and it's very, very important."

"What?"

He held up a menu. "What do you want for breakfast? Your mom said we can get room service!"

After eating and showering, Lindy stood in front of the full-length mirror wearing the suit her mother had bought her for today. It was navy blue and made of scratchy material. The skirt was narrow and went down just past her knees, her hair fell awkwardly against the collar, and the jacket had shoulder pads that made her look like she was wearing a cardboard box. Add to that stockings and a pair of brown shoes with a small heel, and Lindy felt like she was cast as a businesswoman in the school play.

"What do you think?" she asked Tracy, who came out of the bathroom wearing black pants and a sweater. "Mom didn't know what you wear to face the Securities and Exchange Commission."

Tracy raised her eyebrows. "So she figured you should dress like a mini Ms. Hawthorne? Where did she even *buy* that?"

Lindy laughed. "I don't know," she said. "I'm surprised they make things like this in my size. When else would someone my age wear this? To work for a company run by kids?"

"Yeah, it's not like twelve-year-olds go on many job interviews," Tracy said, "for positions in the 1980s."

Their mother came through the door connecting the

suite. She was wearing a suit of her own. "You look perfect, Lindy," she said. "Very appropriate."

"I think you need to call her Melinda in that outfit," Tracy said.

"That's Ms. Sachs to you," Lindy corrected.

Mr. Sachs joined the group in front of the mirror. He was wearing a suit and tie. "Are you ready, Ms. Sachs?"

"Yes," said Mrs. Sachs.

"Yes," said Tracy.

Lindy looked at her reflection and took a big breath. She wished she were going to work at some kid corporation instead of going to do something very adult. But she didn't have a choice. "As ready as I'll ever be."

Chapter 38
Congestion

The traffic got worse as the taxi got closer to the SEC headquarters.

"A little late for rush hour," Mr. Sachs said to the cab driver.

"Eh, DC traffic is terrible always," the cab driver replied. "They have to close streets whenever the president goes somewhere, or the first lady, or some foreign dignitaries."

"Maybe we'll see the motorcade," Tracy said excitedly.

"Maybe," the driver said. "I bet even the president is trying to get to the SEC today. It's all jammed up around there because of the hearing for that stock trading kid."

The three Sachs women looked at one another. *Does he know I'm the stock trading kid?* Lindy wondered. *Or does he think I'm just a regular twelve-year-old in a business suit going to the SEC?*

"But don't worry," the driver said. "I've been driving a cab in DC for twenty-three years. I know all the shortcuts. I'll get you where you need to go."

He maneuvered down alleys and residential streets until they hit a throng of news vans.

"That's the building right there," the driver said. He pointed straight ahead, through the windshield. "I think this is as close as we're going to get. I'm afraid you'll have to walk from here."

"Thank you," said Mr. Sachs. He looked at the meter and took out his wallet.

"Nah," the driver said. "It's on me." He looked over his shoulder at Lindy, who was scooting down the backseat to get out, her skirt getting twisted up. "Good luck," he said to her with a wink.

Out of the cab, Lindy looked down the block, past the mob of reporters and spectators. There was a thick, stately building straight ahead, but that, Lindy realized, wasn't where she was going. The SEC headquarters was on the right, with three flags on tall poles in front. It was a sleek wall of glass that stretched the length of the block, reflecting the street scene and seemingly multiplying the size of the crowd. If she squinted, Lindy could see outlines of people moving around in some of the glass squares. Would her hearing be in a room right on the edge, visible from the ground, so that news crews could point their cameras at her while the reporters guessed at what she was saying? She swallowed, and her throat felt as thick as it had when she had mono.

The four of them walked toward the crowd. It was so packed that Lindy thought they'd have to push their way through, but when they got closer she saw that there were two police officers holding the crowds back so that there was a clear path on the sidewalk and into the building. Lindy knew that the moment they stepped onto that path, flashbulbs and questions would fire. Pretending to be somewhat composed, she straightened her skirt and smoothed her hair.

A young male reporter was the first to spot them. "Melinda Sachs!" he yelled, thrusting a microphone toward her.

Lindy's dad grabbed her right hand, and Lindy grasped her mother's arm with her left. Then Mrs. Sachs took Tracy's arm. The four of them, linked, held tight to one another as they made their way along the length of the building.

Ms. Hawthorne came out from inside to meet them. "Good morning," she said. "You're doing great. Just keep walking."

She opened the door, and the four of them hurried inside. Ms. Hawthorne gave a curt smile to the cameras before she closed the door.

Chapter 39

The Securities and Exchange Commission

The inside of the building was cold and unwelcoming. It was a large, silent atrium with a security desk, conveyor belt, and metal detector, like the world's emptiest airport. The room was all marble and stone, plus a few chairs with leather too sleek to have ever been sat on. A few people in suits scanned their ID badges to pass through glass gates, briefcases in hand. Lindy was instantly glad she'd worn a suit too. She'd have felt even more out of place if she'd been wearing anything else.

When Ms. Hawthorne spoke, the sound bounced harshly off the walls before dissolving into the crisp air. "Francine Hawthorne and the Sachs family," she said, showing her ID to the security guard. "We have a divisional hearing with the Commission."

"I'll need to see IDs from all of you," the guard said lazily, unfazed by the presence of a twelve-year-old in a suit and the multitude of cameras outside.

He took Lindy's and Tracy's school IDs, plus their parents' licenses, and scanned them into his computer. Then he made each of them stand in front of a small camera that was sitting on the counter. He had to angle the camera down for Lindy's turn. She didn't know if she should smile or not, so the photo that was on her temporary visitor badge showed her with an awkward half smile, her eyes pinched with nervousness.

Her badge clipped to the lapel of her suit jacket, Lindy passed through the metal detector and spread her arms so the guard could scan her body with a wand. He did this to everyone, even Ms. Hawthorne, but it still made her feel like she was already found guilty.

"Hearing Room Four," the guard said to Ms. Hawthorne. He pointed toward the elevator, then returned to his seat.

Hearing Room Four was a smaller, simpler, newer version of courtrooms Lindy saw on TV. The setup was the same as a TV courtroom—judge's bench, witness box, tables for the opposing sides—but there was none of the grandeur Lindy had imagined. Everything was made of a crisp gray laminate rather than old, creaky wood. There was a computer in front of where the judge would sit—or, in this case, the five judges; there were five chairs on the platform. *Yesterday it was me against two,* Lindy thought. *Today it's me against five.* But then she looked around her and realized that that wasn't exactly true. Yesterday she'd had Cassie on her side, even if she'd only realized it after the fact. And today she had her whole family and Ms. Hawthorne. She had Cassie, too, even though she wasn't there. She wasn't in this alone.

There was a man to the left of the judges' platform sitting behind of a computer of his own—he was a court stenographer, Lindy realized, there to type up everything she said. There was no jury box, but there were three rows of seats facing the action, which Lindy was relieved to see were empty. Even though Ms. Hawthorne promised the meeting would be private, Lindy had still had nightmares about facing a large, packed courthouse, with people fighting their way for a place in the balcony. There weren't any windows in the room either, Lindy noticed, for the press to be nosy.

Ms. Hawthorne led the family to the table on the far side of the room, facing the judges' bench. There were only three seats there, so they all stood there in silence while Ms. Hawthorne unpacked a big binder from her briefcase. "Mr. Sachs and Lindy will sit up here with me," she said, unloading a stack of papers and placing it on the table next to the binder. "Mrs. Sachs and Tracy, you two can sit behind us"—she gestured to the three rows of empty seats—"since you're not a part of the hearing."

Lindy's mom gave her and her dad a kiss, then squeezed both of their hands. "I'll be right here," she said. She kissed the hands she was squeezing.

"Gosh, Mom," said Tracy. "We're moving two feet away, not to Antarctica."

"I don't care," said Mrs. Sachs. "It *feels* like Antarctica."

"We'll be okay, honey," said Mr. Sachs. "We're glad you're in the audience, though. Right, Lindy Hop?"

Lindy gave her mom a hug. "Yes," she said.

The glass door to the room opened, and a trio of serious-looking people entered: two men and one woman, all in black suits with badges pinned to them, carrying briefcases. They nodded at Ms. Hawthorne, who gave them a polite smile and nodded back.

"Hello, Francine," one of the men said. "Good weekend?"

"Yes, thanks," said Ms. Hawthorne. "And you, Bert?"

"Fine, fine. My son got his learner's permit, so I let him drive around a parking lot while I gripped the side of the car, praying for my life. But fine otherwise."

Ms. Hawthorne chuckled.

Are these the people who've been investigating us? Lindy wondered, wishing she'd paid more attention when Ms. Hawthorne had told her how the hearing would work. They looked like they worked for the SEC, and they were beginning to fill the other desk with thick binders of their own. But she hadn't thought they'd be on such friendly terms with Ms. Hawthorne. She realized now that she hadn't even thought of them as real people, especially real people with teenage sons learning to drive.

Ms. Hawthorne spoke quietly to her and her dad, confirming that they were, in fact, the opposing team. "These are the lawyers from the SEC's Division of Enforcement," she said. "They've been investigating, and they're going to try to convince the Commissioners that there's enough evidence against you to warrant a full trial."

The trio from the Division of Enforcement carried on talking to one another about their children as they settled at their desk.

"The Commissioners will sit up there," Ms. Hawthorne said, pointing to the judges' spot. "They'll hear arguments from both sides and then decide what to do."

Lindy kept her head in the direction Ms. Hawthorne was pointing, but her eyes kept drifting to the Division lawyers. They had an endless number of binders and papers—their desk was filling up—and a young guy in a suit was going in and out of the door, bringing them more.

She glanced down at Ms. Hawthorne's desk, which only had one binder and one stack of papers. What was on all those pieces of paper the Division had? Dug-up evidence about Lindy's life? Detailed law documents? She hoped it wouldn't come down to how much *stuff* each side had, or she and her dad were in for trouble—unless Ms. Hawthorne had a secret stack of binders hidden under her seat, or an assistant of her own to bring some more. She looked over her shoulder to see if Tracy was wondering the same thing, but saw that her sister's eyes were trained not on the papers, but on the guy who was carrying them in. Looking away from the boy for a second, Tracy caught Lindy looking at her and mouthed, "He's cute!"

The clock on the wall hit ten o'clock, and, the moment the second hand clicked over the twelve, a door opened behind the judges' area. Five people—*the* Securities and Exchange Commission—filed out of it and into chairs. They were three women and two men, all wearing black robes. Ms. Hawthorne and the Division lawyers stood up, and Lindy's family followed. Lindy had never sat down, but her heart seemed to fly up to her throat.

"Be seated," one of the women said. She took a seat in

the center. Lindy recognized her from a photo on the SEC's website that was also on the wall in the atrium downstairs. She was the Chairman of the Commission.

Ms. Hawthorne sat down behind her big binder, and she gently touched Lindy's shoulder, motioning for her to sit in the chair next to her.

"Good morning, everyone," the Chairman said as the other Commissioners settled into the chairs on either side of her. Off to the side, the stenographer began typing. "We're here for a preliminary hearing for case number 34-59087, the investigation of Gary M. Sachs and Melinda R. Sachs for alleged insider trading and illegal short selling. May I ask that those present for testimony introduce themselves for the record."

One of the lawyers on the other side, the one whose son was learning to drive, stood and approached the microphone in the center. "Good morning, Commissioners. I'm Bert McDaniel from the Division of Enforcement. I'm joined by my colleagues, Michael Kelly and Norma Winter."

The chairman nodded. Now Ms. Hawthorne stood and approached the microphone. "Good morning," she said. "Francine Hawthorne, representing Gary and Melinda Sachs. Both of my clients are with me this morning."

"Thank you," said the Chairman. Everyone was quiet while she put a small pair of reading glasses on the tip of her nose, shuffled some papers, and examined something on her computer screen. Then she took off the glasses and scanned the people in front of her. Her eyes paused on Lindy, and—so quick Lindy wondered if she'd imagined it—gave her a small wink.

"Okay," the Chairman said. "It is my understanding that the Division of Enforcement has been investigating Mr. Sachs and his daughter for alleged insider trading and illegal short selling, resulting a sale of one thousand shares of Dream Dry stock for a profit of approximately thirty thousand dollars. Is this correct?"

The Division lawyer said, "Yes, your honor."

"And am I correct in stating that the trade was conducted from an online account in Mr. Sachs's name, but the respondents allege that it was Mr. Sachs's daughter Melinda who made the trades?"

"Yes, that's correct," Ms. Hawthorne said.

Your honor, Lindy thought. *She should have said "your honor" like the other guy did.* Ms. Hawthorne was supposed to be one of the leading experts in this, but with her lack of binders and formality, Lindy worried that she even knew what she was doing. She glanced at her dad to see if he was nervous. He was staring at the Commissioners, sitting straighter than a beauty queen.

"Okay," said the Chairman. "Here's what we'll do. The Division will present their opening remarks, and then the respondents will present theirs. Each side will have a chance for rebuttal after that. Okay?"

Ms. Hawthorne nodded. The head Division lawyer said, "Yes, your honor."

"All right," the Chairman said. "Let's begin."

Chapter 40

The Hearing

The man from the Division gathered a stack of papers and stood at the podium, facing the Commission. His hands shook slightly as he tapped them on the table. He was nervous, Lindy could tell, even though he must do this all the time. He cleared his throat and then began reading directly from one of his papers.

"'Good morning, Commissioners,'" he read. "'This morning the Division of Enforcement will demonstrate that Mr. Gary Sachs and his daughter Ms. Melinda Sachs violated the Securities Exchange Act of 1934, Section 10(b), and the Securities Act of 1933, Section 17(a). On the afternoon of January second, an order was placed in Mr. Sachs's online trading account. This order was to short one thousand shares of DDRY, the symbol for the company Dream Dry.

The same account then ended the position less than forty-eight hours later, making a profit of $30.73 per share, or a total of thirty thousand, seven hundred and thirty dollars.'"

Even though this was the most important hour of her life so far, Lindy found it hard to concentrate as the lawyer went on (and on . . . and on . . .). He was telling the story of her day-trading career the way it looked on paper, but he was doing it in such a boring voice and with so many references to various codes and previous legal cases that she could barely keep her eyes open, let alone follow the argument. *Focus,* she told herself, sitting up tall and straightening her jacket. *You're going to have to defend yourself against this guy's claims.* But it was like math class, before Mr. Margolis started to explain things in stock trading terms. She could get it for a few seconds, but the moment her teacher started talking in terms of x and y instead of numbers—or the moment the lawyer started talking in terms of Boesky and Milken and Regulation SHO—her mind started to wander and her posture started to droop. Lindy thought even some of the Commissioners seemed bored. One of the women was pulling lint off her robe, and the man to the far right was studiously picking at his finger.

"In conclusion," the lawyer said after speaking for more than forty minutes, "we in the Division of Enforcement are not convinced that Melinda Sachs"—he nodded at Lindy and gave a small smile, as though her very twelve-year-old presence sealed the case—"made these sophisticated, expensive trades of her own accord. We believe her father made the trades—either directly or via his daughter. Further, we believe that Mr. Sachs had access to insider information regarding Dream Dry that allowed him to act on the tip prior to the public announcement and its effect. Our investigation findings lead us to recommend that the respondents be tried by the Commission." The lawyer looked up from his papers for the first time since he started reading. He cleared his throat once again and said, "Thank you."

The Commissioners shifted in their seats and seemed to regroup.

"Thank you, Mr. McDaniel," the Chairman said. "Ms. Hawthorne," she said, looking at her. "Whenever you're ready."

Ms. Hawthorne stood and replaced the other lawyer at the podium. "Thank you, your honor," she said confidently, and Lindy perked up. Under the table, her dad took her hand.

Lindy thought Ms. Hawthorne did a much better job presenting her argument than the Division guy did. For starters, she didn't just read off a piece of paper. And she didn't reference many codes or cases. What she did do was tell Lindy's story in a conversational yet official way. Lindy found herself nodding along as Ms. Hawthorne recounted the way she started trading, how she lost a lot of money, and how she used the information from Tracy about Dream Dry to make one big, game-changing trade to win it back.

She squeezed her father's hand and examined the faces of the Commissioners as Ms. Hawthorne went along. Were they believing her? Were they hoping she would reference more laws? Why was the man on the far right still picking his finger?

"To conclude," Ms. Hawthorne said, "Melinda Sachs is an intelligent girl who acted on her own free will and got in over her head. Her short sale was based on community gossip, not insider information. She deserves to be tried for her actions—but by Mr. and Mrs. Sachs, not by the SEC. She probably deserves to be punished as well, but given the situation, the sentencing should be left to her parents, not the government. Thank you."

Lindy crossed her fingers. Was that it? Would the Chairman make a decision and that'd be that?

"Thank you, Ms. Hawthorne," the Chairman said. "This isn't your ordinary case." She was quiet for a moment, looking at the people in front of her and pursing her lips. "I'm not sure that I'm interested in hearing rebuttals at this time. What I am interested in is speaking with the respondents—"

Respondents, Lindy thought. *That means me and my dad. We're both going to have to speak.*

"—individually," the Chairman finished.

Lindy's breath caught. Individually? Like, all by herself?

"We'll hear from Mr. Sachs first," the chairman said. "I'll ask Ms."—she glanced down at her notes—"Melinda and her family to please leave the room. I'll have a clerk escort the three of you to the hall, where you'll wait. You may not discuss this case, is that understood?"

Lindy gulped and nodded. Ms. Hawthorne whispered that Lindy should say something. "Yes, your honor," Lindy said, her voice sounding weak.

"Thank you," the Chairman said.

Lindy gripped her dad's hand. They were supposed to be in this together. She didn't want to leave him to face the Commission himself.

"Dad," Lindy whispered.

"It's okay, honey," he said. He gave her a kiss on the cheek. "I'll be okay."

The young guy who'd been carrying the Division's binders appeared at the door to the room, and the Chairman instructed Lindy, her mom, and her sister to go with him into the hall. Ms. Hawthorne gave her a reassuring nod.

Tracy caught Lindy's eye as they walked out of the room. Lindy wondered if her nervous smile was for their dad or the prospect of talking to the cute clerk.

The waiting area turned out to be the couches that were right outside the hearing room. The door was completely soundproof, but her dad was *right* there, which made it more unbearable. The three Sachs women sat together on a sofa, squished up close with Lindy in the middle, even though there was plenty of room. The clerk sat in a chair across from them.

"How are you doing, sweetie?" Lindy's mom asked her.

Lindy shrugged sadly. "Nervous."

"Me too," her mom said.

They both looked in the direction of the hearing room. Mr. Sachs was at the podium and his mouth was moving, but they couldn't make out a single word.

After a full five minutes of silence, Tracy talked to the clerk, trying to be chipper. "So," she said, "you're a clerk?"

"Yep."

"What's your name?"

"Clark," said the clerk.

"Clark," Tracy repeated. "Clark the clerk?"

Lindy asked if she was allowed to go to the bathroom.

Clark the clerk said she could, and he pointed to the door.

She took her time in there, washing her face, staring at herself in the mirror, and taking deep breaths. *You have to do this,* she told herself, *so you might as well do it well.* When she came back, her father was out in the waiting area, having taken her place on the couch.

"How'd it go?" Lindy asked.

"I don't know," Mr. Sachs said, and Lindy could see that he meant it. He looked scared, and he wasn't hiding it very well.

Ms. Hawthorne held open the door to the hearing room. "Lindy," she said gently, "it's your turn."

Chapter 41

Defensive Approach

Lindy stood at the podium. The five Commissioners were lined up in front of her, sitting high on the platform, looking down and straight at her. Even the man on the far right had stopped picking his finger to look at her. Her suit suddenly felt itchier than ever, but she resisted scratching.

Ms. Hawthorne adjusted the microphone down so that it was in the vicinity of Lindy's mouth. Lindy swallowed, and she heard it half a second later, amplified.

"There's no reason to be nervous, Ms. Sachs," the Chairman said. "We just want to hear your side of the story."

Lindy nodded. She knew she should speak—they wouldn't have called her in here, by herself, just to look at her—but she wasn't sure when to start or what to say. She didn't want to break the rules. She looked outside the glass door, at her father. He had his elbows on his knees and his head in his hands. He looked like he might be crying.

"Are you nervous?" the Chairman asked.

Lindy almost laughed. What a ridiculous question. "Yes, your honor," she whispered into the mic. She cleared her throat and then added, a bit louder: "A little."

"Take a few deep breaths," the Chairman said. "And we'll start with some easy questions."

Lindy nodded and gulped again. Following the Chairman's orders, she breathed deeply a few times, making sure to keep her eyes straight ahead so that she didn't have to look at her dad.

"How old are you, Ms. Sachs?" the Chairman asked.

That was an easy one. "Twelve."

"That would put you in . . . sixth grade?"

"Seventh," Lindy said.

"Melinda," the Chairman started. Then she stopped herself. "May I call you Melinda?"

Lindy nodded again. "Or Lindy," she said. "Most people call me Lindy."

The Chairman, and the other Commissioners, smiled. "Lindy," the Chairman said. "How did you get involved in online trading?"

"I had mono," Lindy said. "Mononucleosis," she amended.

She felt her body relax, ever so slightly, as she started to talk. "I was going to be home from school for weeks, or maybe months, and I was bored. My mom and dad said I could do some online trading as a hobby. They gave me a hundred dollars to buy and sell whatever stock I wanted."

One of the other Commissioners spoke. "How did it come about that you wanted to make online trading your hobby?" he asked. "Most seventh graders don't even know what that is."

"I didn't know until I was sick," Lindy said. "First I made a few trades for my dad, because the trading site was blocked at his work. Then I saw how you could make money if you bought and sold things quickly, but he wanted to hang on to his stocks forever—like, for ten years. So when I couldn't go ice-skating, he set me up with my own account and one hundred dollars to buy and sell stuff quickly."

Lindy got more comfortable as she talked, until she almost forgot where she was. She pretended she was talking to Cassie—a more mature, important Cassie who wore a black robe. She continued her story, telling the Commissioners how she started trading in on margin from her dad's account, how she was doing well until she started doing badly. And then how her dad's portfolio started to go down and down and down.

"I shorted Dream Dry," she said, looking straight into the Chairman's eyes. "My sister told me what happened to her friend Leigh Anne's mom, and I remembered reading about how when you short something, you make money if it goes down. So I shorted it to make back everything I lost. And it worked."

"Where did you read about short selling?" one of the female Commissioners asked her.

"In a book my grandma got me," Lindy said. "*Buying Stock for Dummies*."

A few of the Commissioners chuckled.

"You certainly learned a lot from that book," that same Commissioner said. "Enough to become quite an adept day trader. Do you remember reading that short selling can be illegal?" she asked.

Lindy wrinkled her forehead. "It might have said something about it," she admitted. "But I think I skipped that part."

"You *skipped* it," the Chairman repeated, raising her eyebrows.

"Yeah," Lindy said sheepishly. "I skipped anything that seemed boring."

"I'm sure *Buying Stock for Dummies* said something about insider trading," the Chairman said. "I assume you found that part boring too?"

Lindy shrugged one shoulder. "Yeah, I think I skipped that part too."

The Commissioners mumbled and shifted in their seats. At the desk to her right, the lawyers from the Division of Enforcement grumbled.

Lindy knew it sounded unbelievable even as she said it. It would be crazy to think that this girl, standing here awkwardly in an uncomfortable suit, would do what she did. She imagined herself in the Commissioners' position, up there in a black robe, listening to stories from people who broke the law every day, trying to defend themselves. She couldn't imagine any dad breaking the law and trying to get out of trouble by saying his daughter did it, but it probably seemed more imaginable than the daughter actually doing it.

"Your honor," Lindy said. "My dad didn't do anything wrong. It was me. I swear. He didn't even know anything about it. He thought I was just trading with the hundred bucks he gave me. But I got greedy." Her voice caught, but she cleared her throat to stay strong. "I messed up."

The lawyer from the Division of Enforcement stood up. "Commissioners," he said, "with all due respect, do you really believe that this eleven-year-old girl made such sophisticated trades based solely on the 'nonboring' parts of *Stock Trading for Dummies*?"

The Commissioners looked at one another, and Lindy's hands clenched the bottom of her jacket. She thought of yesterday, when she heard Steph telling lies about her, and she'd broken down in front of everyone. This was her chance to stand up for herself, the only chance that really mattered.

Ms. Hawthorne rose, but Lindy spoke before she could. "I did," she said firmly. "Ask my sister, or my math tutor, Mr. Margolis. You can ask my friend Cassie or even my—" she stopped herself from saying "friend"—"this girl, Steph. They all know that I was trading when I was home. *Buying Stock for Dummies* was the most helpful book, but it wasn't the *only* thing I used. I read the *Wall Street Journal* every morning, and I watched CNBC and Bloomberg. I looked at day-trading blogs, and articles, and I got tips from Mr. Margolis. He used to be a stock broker. He taught me how to read the charts on the trading website. The candlestick charts were the best, but the bar charts were good too. I placed stop-losses and limit orders for when I had to go to school and couldn't trade. My dad didn't even know I was trading on margin." She took a deep breath and looked directly at the Division lawyer. "And I'm not eleven. I'm twelve."

Everyone fell silent, and Lindy heard the court stenographer finish typing up her words.

Ms. Hawthorne sat back down.

The Chairman swiveled in her chair to look at her fellow Commissioners. "Does anyone else have any questions for Ms. Sachs at this time?"

None of the commissioners said anything. A couple shook their heads. The man on the end gave her a reassuring smile before looking at his finger, which Lindy imagined must be picked raw.

"Thank you, Ms. Sachs," the Chairman said. "That will be all for now. You may join your family in the waiting area while we hear final statements. We will deliberate after lunch."

That was it, then. Lindy had done all she could, and now she'd just have to wait. She pushed her shoulders back in her suit jacket, stood up as straight as she could, and said, "Thank you."

Chapter 42
The Verdict

The family sat in the waiting area outside Hearing Room Four, staring at one another in silence. Tracy had bitten her nails as short as they could go; Mr. Sachs's hands were rough from rubbing his beard; Mrs. Sachs was sinking into the sofa; and Lindy's suit looked like it'd been crumpled in a suitcase and then put back on. They had braved the barrage of reporters to go out and get some lunch and then again when they came back in. It was now 4:50 p.m., and the Commission was still deliberating. They could keep deliberating until tomorrow morning, or even longer, but Ms. Hawthorne seemed fairly sure that they'd have a decision by the end of the business day, even though that was only ten minutes away. Lindy hoped so.

Clark the clerk opened the door of the hearing room. "Sachses?" he said.

All four of them, plus Ms. Hawthorne, came to life.

"The Commission has reached a decision. You can come back in."

The Sachses looked at one another as they rose. Lindy grabbed both of her parents' hands. They filed back into the hearing room and took the same places as before. The Division lawyers arrived a few minutes later, talking and laughing with one another. Two of them were carrying cups of coffee, and one had a red smoothie. They clearly weren't as stressed about the decision as Lindy and her family.

The door behind the judges' bench opened, and the Commissioners came out as before. The Chairman was holding a small stack of paper. Lindy stood right up.

"Please sit," the Chairman said. She slid her robe underneath her and tapped the papers against the desk. Her eyes did a quick once-over of the crowd before she spoke again. "Thank you for your patience while we discussed the details of this case. Given the evidence at hand and the testimony of the respondents, we have decided that there is no need for further investigation or a trial, civil or criminal."

Lindy inhaled sharply. She looked at Ms. Hawthorne to confirm that meant what she thought it meant. When Ms. Hawthorne smiled—a real, genuine smile—Lindy felt herself burst into a grin. *We won!* she thought. She gripped her father's hand under the desk. It was all she could do to keep from jumping up and down. She wanted to hug everyone— her dad, the Commissioners, even Ms. Hawthorne—but she needed to wait until after the Chairman finished speaking. It was difficult enough to focus on listening, even though the Chairman was saying exactly what she wanted to hear.

Lindy thought, *I did it*. She thought, *They believed me*. But mostly she thought, *Phew*.

"Though we will not bring a suit against either of the respondents," the Chairman continued, "we are hereby ordering that both Mr. Sachs and his daughter cease and desist their trading operations."

"Cease and desist?" Lindy whispered to Ms. Hawthorne.

You're not allowed to do any trading, Ms. Hawthorne wrote on a piece of paper.

No problem! Lindy wrote back. That was fine with her. She drew a smiley face, and Ms. Hawthorne laughed quietly.

"Mr. Sachs," the Chairman said. "You must close your personal online account and refrain from doing any active trading for the next five years. If you wish to invest in the stock market, you may do so through a certified financial adviser or brokerage. Is that understood?"

"Yes, your honor," Mr. Sachs said. "Thank you."

"Lindy," the Chairman said. She took off her glasses and

met Lindy's eyes. "You are clearly a very bright girl. Consider this a very stern warning, and a very, very lucky break. You are not to engage in trading of any sort until you are eighteen years old."

"Yes, your honor," Lindy said, trying not to smile. "Believe me, I won't."

"Good," said the Chairman. "The Commission hereby grants permission to your parents to take up the case from here, and to punish you as they see fit. My guess is that the bill for Ms. Hawthorne's services will be punishment enough. And, Lindy, the next time you decide to play in the big leagues," the Chairman said, a faint smile on her lips, "be sure to read *all* the rules, even the boring ones."

Chapter 43
Options on Futures

It was a week after the hearing, and things were finally starting to feel somewhat normal. Lindy's dad was back at work, the color had returned to her mother's face, and math was once again the most worrisome part of Lindy's life, though it wasn't that worrisome anymore. It helped that she was in the regular class and that Cassie was in it with her. Her parents also let her keep having Mr. Margolis come once a week—they viewed a math tutor as a worthwhile expense, unlike ice-skating or new clothes or a cell phone. Those were things Lindy would have to pay for out of her own money, and it would be a *long* time until she had her own money, since every penny she made from babysitting, raking leaves, and allowance went toward paying for Ms. Hawthorne's services. For representing Lindy and her

ELISSA BRENT WEISSMAN

dad, prepping them for the hearing, and filing all the SEC's paperwork for the investigation, Ms. Hawthorne billed them a whopping thirty-two thousand dollars—two thousand more than Lindy had made in her big, officially *not* illegal, short sale.

"It'd be so easy for you to pay Mom and Dad back if they just let you take *one* TV interview," Tracy said. She, Lindy, and Cassie were hanging out in the living room. Tracy was trying to knit a sock—it was her new hobby.

The mail had just been delivered, and it contained, as it had every day since the hearing, numerous letters from television producers. Lindy's name had stopped making headlines a few days after the verdict, but the offers kept coming.

"They'll pay for TV interviews?" Cassie asked.

"Big bucks," Lindy said. "Same with book deals. But my parents say no. They don't think I should make any money or get more attention for what I did. Which I get. I just wish it would really be over."

"You wish the media would cease and desist?" Tracy asked. That was the new catchphrase in the Sachs house. "I don't. I'm glad the bad parts are over, and the worrying, obviously, but I would totally do a TV interview about it."

"You probably could," Cassie said, "as Lindy's sister."

"Admit it," Tracy said. "I would totally rock it on TV."

Lindy rolled her eyes. "Cease and desist bragging."

The doorbell rang, and the three of them looked at one another. It was the three of them there when the process server had brought the first subpoena, and Lindy hoped, as she rose to answer the door, that this wasn't déjà vu. "Who is it?" she asked.

"Howe," came the reply.

Lindy's mouth dropped open. She raised her eyebrows at Tracy and Cassie.

Tracy pushed herself up from the floor. "I'll leave you three alone," she said, and disappeared down the hall with her yarn and needles.

Lindy opened the door, and sure enough, there was her old friend Howe, who she hadn't spoken to since that terrible morning before the hearing. He'd sent her a few e-mails since, but she hadn't read them. She hadn't deleted them, either; they were just sitting in her in-box, waiting to be opened or trashed. And now here he was outside the glass door, waiting to be invited in or turned away. He had the same round face, the same blue braces, and the same gray windbreaker he always wore. But something about him looked different.

"Hey," Lindy said.

"Hi," said Howe. "Can I come in?"

"Is Steph with you?" Lindy asked.

"No," Howe said. "It's just me."

Lindy reluctantly opened the glass door, and Howe stepped inside but didn't sit down. "Oh hey, Cassie," he said.

"Hi," she said back.

"I'm glad the SEC decided to drop the case," Howe said.

"Me too," said Lindy. She joined Cassie on the couch, leaving Howe standing awkwardly by the door.

"I'm sorry I was a jerk," Howe said. "While you were, you know, dealing with everything."

Lindy didn't say anything. She loved being friends with Cassie, and maybe that was all she needed. But, good or bad, she'd lost Steph, and seeing Howe made her realize that she didn't want to lose him too. She missed him.

"I'm sorry Steph was a jerk too. I think she was just sad that you guys weren't hanging out anymore, but she shouldn't have said that stuff."

Lindy crossed her arms. If Steph really was sad about their friendship, she had a strange way of showing it. And Steph wasn't the one apologizing for herself, but then again, if she were, would Lindy have even let her in? The truth was that Steph had sent her an e-mail too, shortly after the verdict of her hearing made the news. That one Lindy had deleted without even checking to see if it contained an apology.

"I think she misses you. I mean," Howe said, "I miss you. And I wanted to tell you that Steph and I broke up."

Lindy and Cassie looked at each other.

"It really wasn't cool what she said to you."

"No, it wasn't," Lindy agreed.

"Well," Howe said. He sighed. "I just wanted to say I'm sorry and say that I'll see you in school." He looked at her for a second, then suddenly remembered something. "Oh!" He fumbled inside his backpack, then held out a squished cupcake in a plastic bag. "I brought you this. It's a Mohawk cupcake. I saved it from lunch."

Lindy couldn't help but smile, or marvel at how Howe had been able to not eat it and save it for her. "Thanks," she said, taking the bag from him.

"All right," Howe said. "I'm going to go home. Maybe I'll see you online tonight?"

Lindy nodded. "Okay. See you later."

Howe adjusted his backpack, relieved. "Okay!" he said, a little too excited. "Bye, Lindy." He opened the door.

"Bye, Howe," Cassie called.

"Bye, Cassie," he said. "Bye, Lindy." He waved awkwardly and closed the door.

Lindy and Cassie looked at each other and laughed.

Cassie said, "That was nice. Do you think you guys'll be friends again?"

"I hope so," Lindy said honestly. She shrugged. "We'll see, I guess."

Tracy poked her head into the living room. She said, "Can I have some of that cupcake?"

As she got napkins and a knife, Lindy noticed the time. Four p.m.: time for the stock market's closing bell. It was nice to not have to worry about that. Maybe she'd talk to Howe online later. Maybe she'd take a peek at the *Wall Street Journal*, too, just to see what was going on in the market. Who knows—she might someday get back in the trading game. Or maybe she'd become a securities attorney like Ms. Hawthorne, or even work for the SEC. Maybe one day she'd be a rich business tycoon, like that quiz she'd taken said, or maybe she'd take that book deal when she was older, and she'd become a bestselling author.

But for now, all four p.m. meant was that her mom would be home any minute, and her dad would follow at six. And right now, she was happy just to have this cupcake, split three ways.

Acknowledgments

Writing is a solitary endeavor, yet this book wouldn't exist without the help of so many wonderful people. Many thanks to Robert Heim of Meyers & Heim LLP, who took the time to speak with me, answer my many questions, and share his expertise on Securities Law. I often say that I know a story is working when a character gets into a situation that I don't know how to get her out of. Lindy got herself into some major trouble, and Mr. Heim helped show me her way out.

Thanks, too, to the SEC for their comprehensive, endlessly helpful website, and for allowing me to visit and sit in on an administrative hearing. It's not often I get to do research of this sort, and I truly appreciate the SEC being so accommodating.

I hope Lindy came off as having a deeper understanding of the stock market than I have. For this I must acknowledge Ken Little's *The Complete Idiot's Guide to Active Trading* and investopedia.com. I hope readers with more knowledge will respect the creative liberties I've taken with the business of etrading and be willing to forgive my mistakes.

A million thanks to the extraordinary Flip Brophy and Julia Kardon, who make all this possible. At Atheneum, this book was made infinitely better by the insightful, supportive wisdom of Rūta Rimas, who loved Lindy and her antics the way only a math-teacher-turned-editor could. A big thanks to everyone at Simon & Schuster who worked on this book, especially Christina Solazzo, whose copyediting went above and beyond (and involved a number of impressive mathematical charts!). Thanks, too, to the many editors I've had the privilege of working with over the past few years. All of them have helped me grow as a writer and have provided invaluable encouragement that's kept me going.

Speaking of encouragement, thank you to my students, who inspire me every semester, and the kids who read my books and remind me that I've got the best job in the world. And to the authors whose books I grew up reading that made me want to write, and whose ranks I still can hardly believe I've joined. Saving the best for last, thank you to my family: my parents, grandparents, brothers, and all of the Roches, especially Grant, Karina, and Lev.